Please turn to the back of the book for a conversation between Judy...

D1193757

Praise for Judy Fitzwater's previous Jennifer Marsh mysteries

Dying to Get Even

"One of the funniest new mystery authors since Janet Evanovich."
—*Meritorious Mysteries*

"Fitzwater once again offers an entertaining read."
—*Publishers Weekly*

"In *Dying to Get Even* are the seeds of a very funny parody of genre writing. . . . Jennifer and her friends are a genial bunch—and one can't help but root for them."
—*Rock Hill Herald* (SC)

Please turn the page for more reviews. . . .

Dying to Get Published

"A sprightly novel . . . It offers a word to the wise: Never thwart a mystery writer, published or unpublished."
—CAROLYN HART

"Enjoyable reading for writers hoping to break into the mystery field."
—*Ellery Queen's Mystery Magazine*

"In a roller coaster of hilarity, Fitzwater has crafted three-dimensional characters with warmth, realism, and wickedness."
—*The Snooper*

Dying to Get Published

"Fitzwater provides an entertaining (and for aspiring writers, frustratingly familiar) look at the world of writing and publishing."
—*Publishers Weekly*

"Expertly plotted . . . Ingenious and satisfying."
—*The Mystery Review*

By Judy Fitzwater
Published by The Ballantine Publishing Group:

DYING TO GET PUBLISHED
DYING TO GET EVEN
DYING FOR A CLUE

Books published by The Ballantine Publishing Group
are available at quantity discounts on bulk purchases
for premium, educational, fund-raising, and special
sales use. For details, please call 1-800-733-3000.

DYING FOR A CLUE

Judy Fitzwater

FAWCETT CREST • NEW YORK

A Fawcett Crest Book
Published by The Ballantine Publishing Group
Copyright © 1999 by Judy Fitzwater

All rights reserved under International and Pan-American Copyright Conventions. Published in the United States by The Ballantine Publishing Group, a division of Random House, Inc., New York, and simultaneously in Canada by Random House of Canada Limited, Toronto.

Fawcett is a registered trademark and Fawcett Crest and the Fawcett colophon are trademarks of Random House, Inc.

www.randomhouse.com/BB/

Library of Congress Catalog Card Number: 99-90466

ISBN 0-449-00426-0

Manufactured in the United States of America

First Edition: October 1999

10 9 8 7 6 5 4 3 2 1

For Larry

I couldn't write without the help and support of the talented people who surround me:

My husband, Larry, and daughters, Miellyn and Anastasia, who are not only my personal cheering section but also the source of many wonderful suggestions, not to mention free editing services.

My weekly critique group: Robyn Amos, Barbara Cummings, Ann Kline, Vicki Singer, and Karen Smith, who are invaluable for their honest criticism and incredible creativity.

My terrific editor, Joe Blades, who continues to help me learn this business with great good humor (and who, I only wish, could publish the books that Jennifer writes).

Patricia Peters, Joe's assistant, who brings with her enthusiastic support and skillful editing.

Dr. Bruce Goldin, who supplied me with information about heterochromia.

George W. McGuire III, for his knowledge of Macon, Georgia.

And Bob Bockting, always helpful with his suggestions and comments.

DYING FOR
A CLUE

Prologue

Lazy jazz swelled in the background as Jennifer Marsh looped the belt of her tan trench coat and cinched it tightly against her thin waist. She opened a tube of lipstick and rouged her lips. Then she tucked her long, taffy brown hair behind her ears, ran her hand over the crease of the brown fedora, and placed it on her head, tugging it snugly over one arched eyebrow. She raised the collar of her coat, drew on a pair of thin, synthetic calfskin gloves, and winked at her reflection in the dresser mirror.

Murder was about to become her business.

Chapter 1

The alley behind the short side of the L-shaped strip of shops and offices on Macon's southern side was dark, dirty, and rank, and Jennifer had just about had it with playing detective. The last ten minutes had held none of the dark, brooding atmosphere of a Philip Marlowe novel nor the cool sophistication of Lawrence Sanders' Archy McNally. She was hot and muggy, she was bored, and she felt gypped.

Crouching behind a stack of cardboard boxes, staring at two delivery men whispering to someone at the back entrance to the East Lake Fertility Clinic was hardly what she'd had in mind when she signed on as Johnny Z's assistant. She didn't even know who the men were or why they would be making deliveries on a Sunday night, and every time she tried to ask Johnny, he'd shushed her. All he told her was they were to pick up some material for a client.

She glanced over at the lean, wiry form hunched behind one of the larger boxes. She'd had great hopes for him. If she squinted just right and looked at him out of the corner of one eye, he bore a remarkable resemblance to Humphrey Bogart. But right now he seemed as bored as she was, cleaning his nails with a large pocketknife.

Then one of the delivery men shouted something and

dropped down. His hand went to his back pocket, and a woman screamed. A loud pop echoed down the alley.

Jennifer jerked back. The box she was hiding behind shifted, and Johnny's knife clattered to the pavement. The man turned in their direction.

The next bullet clipped past Jennifer's ear, leaving her temporarily deaf on her right side. Instinctively, she rolled, tumbling painfully into the brick wall of the alley and into shelter behind a Dumpster. She felt the sleeve of her trench coat tear across her aching shoulder.

"Oh my God," she wailed, more a prayer than a curse. "They're *shooting* at us." She was shaking so badly she could barely pull herself up.

Johnny Z was still hunched behind the boxes, but cardboard offered only psychological protection against bullets, and if he didn't bail quickly . . .

Another bullet tore past, and this one left a dark trail as it skidded across the asphalt. Johnny Z crumpled backward, and Jennifer watched in horror as a dark pool seeped beneath him. He'd better not die on her. She had a few choice words she wanted to say to him first.

She was desperate to escape but knew she couldn't outrun anyone, especially not in her current jellylike state.

She dragged herself up against the Dumpster, found a foothold on the side of the bin and dove, headfirst, into something squishy, and worse, smelly. She'd worry about what disease she'd catch later—if there was a later. She sucked in one great nauseating gulp of air, her heart straining against her rib cage. It would be nice to stop breathing altogether, but last time she checked, it was a requirement for living.

She waded back under the cover, closed her eyes, and prayed—prayed for Johnny Z, the third-rate private detective whose lifeblood was staining some grimy alley in

Macon, Georgia, and prayed for her overly ambitious and overly stupid self.

What a revolting situation for an unpublished crime writer—*fictional* crime, Jennifer reminded herself. Doing some practical research for her novels had seemed like such a good idea. But did that mean she had to hook up with some guy she found in the phone book—the last name listed under INVESTIGATORS—and the only one willing to let her tag along after him?

They'd find her body in the morning. Riddled with bullets, alongside Johnny Zeeman's. Or suffocated amid a Chinese restaurant's garbage, the victim of noxious fumes. Dead. And she wouldn't even know why.

Poor Sam. He might even be the one to identify her corpse, sent to the scene to cover the story for *The Macon Telegraph*. He'd take it hard. They were close even if they did share a kind of limbo relationship because of her obsession with becoming a published novelist.

Ever since he'd helped her clear her name in the Penney Richmond murder, they'd been more or less a couple: him being the more, her the less. She had real feelings for him, but she needed time to sort them out. Unfortunately, time was something she might well be fresh out of.

She heard two sets of footsteps running toward her.

"Where'd the other one go?" a man asked.

"Must have run off," a second voice suggested.

"Check the Dumpster."

Jennifer froze. If God was with her, they wouldn't have a flashlight. She heard a foot hit the metal support she'd used to push herself high enough to climb in.

A nearby voice said, "Man, you've got to be kidding. No one would hide in that stinking mess."

Jennifer heard him push off, his shoes hitting the pavement, and she allowed herself to breathe again. Bad idea.

"Come on," the other man called. She listened as the two sets of footsteps hurried back up the alley. An engine started, followed by what sounded like a truck pulling away.

What seemed like an eternity passed. Jennifer opened one eye and then the other. The ringing in her ear had now softened to a dull throb.

They were gone. Maybe they wouldn't come back.

She raised her head and strained to hear. She needed to check on Johnny Z. Her muscles twitching wildly, Jennifer popped her head out of the bin. Ah! Fresh air—at least relatively speaking.

The alley was silent. She heard nothing and saw nothing, except for Johnny's body lying a few yards away.

She'd have to chance it. She hoisted herself up onto the lip of the bin, threw one leg over the side, and lowered herself to the ground. She was covered, head to toe, in yuck, her precious brown fedora forever lost. Ducking down, she scurried to Johnny's side.

His eyes were closed, and a small patch of blood discolored the shoulder of his shirt. She bent over him and lightly touched his craggy cheek, a great sob welling in her throat. "Oh, Johnny," she whispered, as though she'd known him much longer than two days. Her tears splashed onto his nose. "I'm so very—"

Suddenly, Johnny's eyes popped open. "What the hell is that godawful smell?"

"You're alive!" Jennifer shrieked in good Frankenstein fashion, jerking backward.

"I am now. Whatever you're wearing is a lot more powerful than smelling salts. Are they gone?"

She nodded frantically, as much to reassure herself as him.

Johnny tried to move his arm but stopped, gasping.

"There's a cell phone in my inside jacket pocket. Call 911 before I bleed to death."

She groped for the phone, found it, and dropped it.

"Don't break the blasted thing," Johnny chastised.

She peeled off her gloves, which were covered in something resembling duck sauce, scooped up the phone, and made the call with fingers that felt like concrete.

"They'll be here in about five minutes," she assured Johnny.

"Good. How many shots did you count?" he asked.

"Three."

"That's what I thought. Check it out. See where the first one went."

"Me?" she asked incredulously.

"What? You expect me to get up and leak blood halfway up the alley to see who else went down?"

"I don't know. How bad are you hurt?"

"Do it, Marsh," Johnny ordered.

Well, this was what she'd come for, wasn't it? To find out what it was like to be a *real* detective.

She shed the coat, folding it neatly inside out, and laid it on the pavement. September in Georgia, even on a cool night, was too hot for it anyway.

Johnny made an impatient motion, and she stood up. "All right, already. I'm going."

Quietly she covered the fifty feet to the back entrance of the clinic, fully aware that she was in the open and there were no handy Dumpsters to provide shelter should the gunmen return.

The door was standing open, light illuminating the narrow, brightly white hallway. She inched forward. Did she really have to do this? She should be home writing, not running around in some dingy alley looking for who knew what. But she couldn't just leave. Someone inside might need help, and, unfortunately, she was the only able-bodied person on the scene. Even if she did get sick at the sight of blood.

She cursed her own cowardice, threw back her shoulders, and plunged forward.

Just inside, she found a woman, sitting in a pool of blood, slumped awkwardly against the wall. Jennifer bent down next to her and gently lifted her chin. Two round eyes stared up at her, wide open. There was a small hole in the woman's neck.

The eyes. Large, beautifully shaped, tilted like almonds and fringed with long lashes. Startling. Arresting. Unnatural. One blue, one brown. Jennifer felt somehow confused. As if she couldn't quite make sense of what she was seeing. As if her own eyes were betraying her.

For a moment she swayed back on her feet. The light in the hallway seemed to grow bright and then to dim. Blue mixed with brown, brown with blue, until she wasn't sure what she saw. Her head became light, and she lost her sense of up and down. She felt like she was falling, then tumbling into the whirlpool of those stone-cold, dead eyes.

Chapter 2

Her right cheek stung and then her left. Jennifer opened her eyes just in time to flinch from the back of a large hand threatening to land yet another blow.

"She's awake," the man squatting in front of her announced. "I don't see any wounds, but I still haven't figured out what happened to her. She looks like she's been slimed." Turning back to Jennifer, he asked, "Are you hurt?"

This from some baby-faced cop who was slapping her mercilessly? She scowled, rubbed her cheek, and pulled her legs up under her. There was hardly room for one person in the narrow hallway, let alone half a dozen.

"Sorry, ma'am—about your cheek," he added.

The Big Three-O was bearing down on her, but Jennifer hardly considered herself a *ma'am*. The word stung more than the slap.

She shook her head. Except for a crick in her neck from the way she'd fallen when she fainted, the muddle where her brain should be, and the fact that she smelled like a sewer, she was doing great.

The policeman helped her to her feet. Her hip ached and her knee almost gave way when she put her weight on it. Maybe she wasn't so all right after all. She bit her lip and hoped he wouldn't notice. All she wanted was out of there.

A paramedic was bending over the other woman, fortunately shielding Jennifer from those wide-open, blank eyes.

"She's dead, isn't she?" Jennifer asked, keeping her own eyes steadfastly on the man next to her.

"Oh, yeah," the policeman assured her, shuffling her outside, his arm securely supporting her. Police cars, blue lights flashing, blocked her view of either end of the alley. He pulled her toward an ambulance waiting near the door, but she balked.

"I think it'd be better if you went to the hospital and let them check you out," he insisted.

"No, I'm fine. How's Johnny Z?"

"You mean Mr. Zeeman, the man we found up the way?"

She nodded.

"They've already taken him in. He was lucid. Lost a bit of blood, but I think he'll be all right."

Good! Then he'd feel it when she strangled him. Johnny Z had said nothing about guns or bullets—or dying—when he'd invited her along. A simple case. Hah! People didn't get shot over a simple anything.

Jennifer licked her lips. This whole P.I. business was tasting pretty sour about now.

"Where'd they take him?"

"Macon General."

She started off down the alley.

"We need to talk to you," the policeman insisted, following her.

She spun on her heels and almost bumped into him. "You said I should go to the hospital. You can talk to me there."

It was fortunate he'd called her ma'am and that he was younger than she was. It made it a whole lot easier to flout her ingrained respect for the law and march, with only a slight limp, straight up that alley toward her car and through a news crew from Channel 14.

When they finally wheeled Johnny Z into his room, he looked at least ten years older than the forty or so Jennifer guessed him to be. He was ashen and looked more like he belonged in the morgue than in a hospital. But then, the couple of times she'd seen him, he hadn't looked much better.

His shoulder was swathed in gauze. The bullet had gone straight through, Jennifer could testify to that, so the doctors had been left with clean-up and patch-up.

Two nurses fussed over him, adjusting his IV, and then left.

"Does it hurt much?" Jennifer asked.

Johnny shifted and winced. "How'd you get in here?" Obviously he was too tough to grouse about his wounds.

She took the chair next to the bed. "I simply kept my eyes forward and acted like I knew what I was doing."

He nodded. "Usually works."

"That—and I'm now your niece, your only living relative."

"Welcome to the family."

She ignored the leer in his watery eyes.

"You know, when you didn't come back, I thought somethin' might've happened to you," he said softly.

Sentimental? Johnny? Could it be he was having an attack of conscience for taking her with him? Hah! She hardly thought so.

"You in a lot of pain?" she asked again.

"Not particularly. Who took the bullet?"

"A short woman with the most incredible eyes."

"Damn," he cursed.

"You know her?" Jennifer asked.

"Yeah, you know her, Zeeman?" It was a big, middle-aged man in a suit with the baby-faced cop. They were standing in the doorway.

"I don't know. Could be my client, Diane Robbins."

"Guess you won't be getting your bonus," the older man suggested, grinning smugly.

"Bonus?" Jennifer asked.

"Zeeman here takes a bullet, and he gets an extra five hundred dollars, plus hospital expenses, on top of his daily fee while recovering."

Could that be why Johnny waited too long to get out of the line of fire? Nah. Surely not. No one would—

"It's in his standard contract. Part of the fine print. How much you made off that clause now? Three, four thousand maybe?" the man asked, sizing up Jennifer as he approached the bed.

She felt at a distinct disadvantage. Although she'd stopped at the rest room, paper towels only went so far getting Dumpster crud out of hair.

"So, niece, you got a name?"

"Jennifer Marsh," she offered.

She could tell from his smirk he already knew who she was. He offered his hand. "Lieutenant Schaeffer, Macon police. You're the one who made the 911 call."

She nodded. This nice-looking lieutenant had an easy, friendly manner, but she knew to be wary. She felt like she'd done something wrong even if she had no idea what it was.

He turned around a straight-back chair, sat, then stuck a toothpick into his mouth and proceeded to chew on it. "So tell me, Johnny. What happened in that alley?"

Jennifer crossed her arms and leaned back. Schaeffer had asked the question she wanted answered.

Johnny shook his head. "Hey, man, you know about as much as I do. All I know is five days ago this Robbins woman comes into my office, requesting my services. Young. Good-lookin'."

Jennifer rolled her eyes. Sheesh! This guy was acting like he'd crawled out of the pages of a Sam Spade novel. The next thing she knew, he'd be saying she was wearing one of those little pillbox hats with black netting on it.

Zeeman shrugged his shoulders and let out a painful-sounding gasp. "She said she needed my help. All I know is, I was to pick up something at the back door of the East Lake Fertility Clinic, but these two punks in a delivery truck showed up. I was waiting for them to leave when all hell broke loose."

Schaeffer took the toothpick out of his mouth and pointed it at Zeeman as if it were a lethal weapon. "Don't play cute with me," he warned. "You're not as stupid as you look."

Now both of them were doing it. But she could sympathize. If she'd had a rubber hose, she would have handed it to Schaeffer.

"Could we just cut to the chase?" she begged.

They ignored her.

"I swear. That was all there was to it. She said she didn't want to plant no ideas in my head."

Why not? Apparently there was plenty of room.

"I was to collect some envelope and deliver it to her. End of story."

Schaeffer drew a bead on Jennifer. "That sound familiar to you?"

She pursed her lips. "He's told you more than he ever told me."

"Just what the hell were you doing in that alley with Zeeman anyway?" he demanded.

She opened her mouth but stopped short. Right now the whole mystery writer business seemed even more ludicrous than it had in the alley with bullets whizzing past. She cleared her throat and pasted on her most naive smile. "You're probably not going to believe this, and even if you do—"

"She's my new partner," Johnny interrupted. "I was training her."

Her mouth dropped open. Technically, she supposed, she could view that comment as an offer of employment.

Schaeffer shook his head at her, stood up, and kicked the chair out of the way. "You look like a nice young woman. Find yourself another line of work."

She nodded, in total agreement.

Schaeffer took her elbow. "Come on," he said, pulling her out of her chair.

"Where?" she sputtered.

"I need your statement."

"But—"

"Now." He towed her toward the door.

"But—" she repeated, twisting back to see the smirk on Johnny Z's face. Schaeffer had her almost out the door before she managed to shout out, "I quit!"

Chapter 3

Beeeep!

Jen, it's Teri. Where the heck are you? And what were you doing in some alley in the middle of the night? Can't you be left alone for one minute? I caught your little appearance on the eleven o'clock news. That was you, wasn't it, pushing your way through those reporters? Don't make me come find you. Call me!

Beeeep!

Sweetie, it's Leigh Ann. What have you got yourself into this time? And what happened to your hair? Did you meet that new cutie they've got doing the location shoots for Channel 14? He is sooooo hot! Makes me want to ... Anyway, call me!

Beeeep!

Jennifer, you there, hon? Are you trying to scare me into labor? Not that that would be a bad thing. I'm more than ready for this baby to be born. Hope you're all right. It's April, but then you knew that.

Beeeep!

Jennifer, call me when you get in. It's Monique.

Well, they'd all just have to wait. It was way too late to call anyone, and would have been even if she'd noticed the blinking light on her answering machine when she first dragged in after her visit with Lieutenant Schaeffer. They'd all seen her on TV, so her writing buddies at least knew she was alive. She'd explain later, as much later as she could get away with. Besides, what she needed right now was to relax.

Jennifer rewrapped the towel that kept threatening to fall off her wet hair, snuggled down in her terry-cloth robe as she sank onto her couch, and warmed her hands with the mug of hot chocolate she'd brought from the kitchen. It smelled yummy, and it didn't ask questions. Or talk back. She took a long, creamy sip.

She propped her bare feet on the coffee table and rubbed Muffy's ears. At least the dog was behaving again. When she'd gotten home, Muffy had been all over her as if she were a doggy smorgasbord. Guess her dog liked Chinese.

But now that Jennifer was clean, finally clear of every last dab of Dumpster goo and sufficiently groomed, Muffy had returned to her normal, greyhound self: a sponge for attention.

She sighed. She'd done it again, plunged headlong into one heck of a mess, and all for the sake of her writing. She allowed herself a small grin. After all, she had survived through her own resourcefulness. And she'd endured a real-life shootout. Her first. Hopefully, her only.

She patted her tummy. Someday she'd tell Jaimie, her yet-to-be-conceived child, all about it. How his or her mother had bravely withstood a barrage of gunfire. How she had watched a fellow private eye take a bullet, and then how she had sought refuge . . . Jennifer screwed up her face. Maybe it would be better not to tell all of this particular story.

At least she'd made it out in one piece, unscathed, which meant that Jaimie might actually have a chance of someday being conceived and born—born to his or her mystery-writer mother.

She blew on the hot chocolate and enjoyed a healthy

gulp. She was safe, Johnny would recover, Schaeffer was satisfied she would be of no more help to him, and she could get on with her life—her *real* life as a writer, which, if a bit uneventful, was looking pretty attractive about now.

A soft knock fell on the front door of her apartment. She jumped, splashing some of the hot chocolate onto her thumb, which she promptly stuck in her mouth. She checked her watch. It was after one A.M. Who the heck would be knocking on her door at this hour?

Muffy woofed and looked up at her expectantly. She put a calming hand on the dog's neck, but the next thud sent her barking and scurrying for the door. Reluctantly, Jennifer followed.

It must be Sam. One of his fellow reporters could have called him about what went down in the alley, or maybe he caught the news and was there to check on her. He'd probably be a tiny bit irritated that she hadn't called him herself. She had every intention of doing so, but in the morning—after she'd figured out a way to tell him about Johnny Z that wouldn't launch a barrage of reproaches. Sam couldn't possibly come up with any she hadn't already told herself. Still, it was sweet of him to come by.

She adjusted the towel on her head and looked through the peephole.

But it wasn't Sam standing in the dim light. The figure was dark in the shadow, small and definitely female. The woman knocked again and whispered loudly, "Marsh, let me in! Johnny Zeeman sent me."

Terrific. Johnny wasn't exactly at the top of her most popular list at the moment, and she certainly had no desire to meet any of his friends.

"Marsh," the woman called again, banging loudly with her forearm and without even enough courtesy to add a Ms. to the front of her name. "You have to—"

Jennifer jerked open the door and pulled the woman inside. She didn't need another visit with the police. Mrs. Thorne down the hall had 911 on her speed dial.

She clutched the terry-cloth robe tightly across her chest and demanded, "What?"

The woman looked startled, her big, dark brown eyes, outlined in heavy black, as wide as if Jennifer had started the ruckus herself.

Jennifer looked her up and down. She was nicely rounded, dressed in tight black pants with a black turtleneck covered by a brown leather jacket. The woman stood at least three inches shorter than her own five-foot-six. With her dark, chin-length hair raked back with a headband and shining an unnatural red, she had to be a teenager. No one else dyed their hair that color. She even had a kind of dewy-eyed look amid all that eyeliner.

But whatever her age, she could certainly use a lesson in manners. One didn't go knocking on a stranger's door in the middle of the night.

Muffy whimpered and wedged herself between the two women.

"They killed her," the girl gasped out. "I saw it on the news. God, they actually killed her." She swayed and, for a moment, Jennifer was afraid she was going to collapse. Jennifer grabbed her elbow, but the girl jerked back out of her grasp.

"I called all the hospitals until I finally found Johnny." The girl's face seemed an unnatural white, either from the contrast with the hair or from fear. It was impossible to tell which. "He told me to come to you. That you'd take care of it."

At the moment, all Jennifer wanted to take care of was Johnny Z. She certainly didn't have time for babysitting, and whatever this gal needed or wanted, she was definitely in the wrong place.

The girl licked her dark red lips and asked, "Did you get it?" She tucked back her hair, revealing tiny hoops and studs that outlined the entire edge of her ear.

"Who *are* you?" Jennifer demanded.

The girl started to speak and then stopped, as though catching herself. "They call me Diane Robbins."

Jennifer blinked hard. This girl must be Johnny's client, the one that supposedly took that first bullet in the alley. It was hardly a natural mistake. She'd described the victim as petite with big eyes, both of which fit. She hadn't mentioned middle-aged, blond, and conservatively groomed. She'd had trouble getting past those eyes.

"Did you get it?" the girl repeated, more agitated this time.

"Get what?" Jennifer asked.

"The envelope."

"I don't know what you're talking about. I don't work for Johnny Zeeman, despite what he told you. No one gave me anything."

This conversation was getting more convoluted by the minute. Unfortunately, only one of them seemed to know what they were talking about, and that someone wasn't her. She had nothing to offer this girl, except a little advice. "You need to talk with someone who can actually help you—like the police."

Jennifer put her hand on the doorknob, but the girl brushed past her, plopped onto the couch, and stuck her booted feet up on the coffee table. Loudly, Jennifer cleared her throat and stood her ground.

The girl crossed her arms. "I'm not leaving until you tell me what I want to know. You were with her when she died—Johnny told me so. If she didn't give you the information, you can at least tell me what she said."

"You mean the woman at the clinic? She was already dead when I got to her."

"Oh, no. You're not getting away with that. She promised to give Johnny the material. She *must* have said something, and I want to know what it was."

A tremor started in her chin, and tears were beginning to make her eyeliner pool. Maybe this girl wasn't quite as cocksure as she'd wanted her to believe.

"She had a bullet hole in her throat," Jennifer said, as gently as she could manage. "Even if she'd been alive, which she wasn't, she wouldn't have been able to talk. Whatever business you have with Johnny Z, you'll have to take up with him, Miss Robbins."

"Don't call me that!" The girl stood and flew at her, her face suddenly contorted with rage.

Jennifer held her ground. "Didn't you just tell me your name was Diane Robbins?"

The girl balled her hands into fists and, for a moment, Jennifer was convinced she was going to have to defend herself.

"Don't you see? That's the whole point." The girl's voice broke and her body sagged, all of the fight gone out of her. "I don't know who I am."

Chapter 4

"Let me get this straight," Jennifer said after she managed to get Diane back to the safety of the sofa. "You're not actually Diane Robbins?"

"No, I'm not," the girl declared defiantly, as if Jennifer had intended to argue with her about it.

"And you don't know who you are?"

The girl nodded vigorously.

"Think you could help me out here a little?" Jennifer asked. If the girl was suffering from amnesia, that would be one thing, but she seemed neither confused nor disoriented. And she certainly couldn't have managed that eye makeup if she'd been either. No, she was angry.

"If this story has a beginning," Jennifer said, "I would appreciate hearing it."

"Didn't Johnny tell you?"

Jennifer shook her head, and the towel fell off. She dumped it on the floor, and Muffy immediately nested in it. Her hair would just have to dry naturally. She'd fight with it in the morning. And she was way too tired to wrestle with Muffy over the towel tonight.

"Johnny doesn't talk much," Jennifer explained. "At least not to me. He told me nothing about you. All I know is that he was supposed to pick up something from the woman at the clinic. What was it?"

Diane shook her head and stuck out her chin. "If I knew that, I wouldn't be here."

Jennifer sighed. Diane wasn't any easier to talk to than Johnny. "Who made the contact with the woman at the clinic?" Maybe she'd do better answering direct questions.

"I found her, but Johnny set up the meeting. Valerie and me were exploring Macon, and we kind of got lost on the south side of town. We finally stopped at a little shopping area, looking for a phone to call somebody to see if we could get directions back to campus."

"What campus?"

"Lanier. She and me are freshmen there."

Jennifer nodded, hoping she wasn't an English major. "So you were looking for a phone . . ."

"Yeah, and we found one in front of this Chinese restaurant. Valerie was calling, only nobody was in their rooms, so I wandered down the way to see what was in the center. And that's when I saw it. I almost *died*."

"Saw what?"

"The clinic." She said it as though she thought Jennifer was stupid.

"But why did that upset you?"

"I don't know." She shook her head. Her voice choked up again, and she blanched an alarming shade of pale. She seemed so young, so vulnerable under all that make-up. Jennifer reached out a hand to her, but she shrugged it off and sat up straight.

"It looked familiar to me, you know? But it was a bad kind of familiar, a kind of sick-to-my-stomach familiar. I don't think I've ever been so freaked out in my life." Even now her hands shook, just talking about it.

"I guess Valerie thought I was going to pass out. My legs started to give way. She left me and ran inside to get some help. A nurse came out, the one that died. She came over to me and reached down to pull me up and that's when I saw them. She had the weirdest eyes, one blue, one brown. And I guess that's when I fainted."

Terrific. She hoped all this was making more sense to Diane than it was to her. "So you see this nurse and you faint."

"Dead away."

"And then?"

"I couldn't have been out more than a minute or two. I woke up *inside* the clinic, in one of those awful, sterile examining rooms, like something out of *One Flew over the Cuckoo's Nest* where they fried that guy's brain. That same nurse was holding some foul-smelling stuff under my nose. I grabbed her arm and said, 'I know you.' She just stared at me. Another woman came in and said the doctor would be in in a minute. All I knew was I had to get the hell out of there. No way I was waiting for some doctor, not in that place."

"So you left."

"I grabbed Valerie and we ran. But I'd seen her name tag. B. Hoffman. We took off driving until we found the interstate. When I got back to the dorm, I called every private investigator in the phone book. The only one that would help me without money up front was Johnny Zeeman."

Seemed like Johnny was everybody's last resort. "So what did you tell him?"

"What I told you—that and the fact that I know I've been there before, a long, long time ago, and that it made me really, really scared. I want to know why."

"But what does all this have to do with your not being Diane Robbins?"

"I called my mom and told her about finding the clinic and that I'd contacted Johnny. She made this kind of gurgling sound over the phone. And then she said something like, 'How could you possibly remember?' And when she said that, I knew."

"Knew what?"

"That she wasn't my mother, not my real mother."

Whoa. The girl had just lost her again. "Not your mother?" Jennifer repeated. "How—"

"I don't know. I just knew. She insisted that I come home. I told her no way. She started crying. She kept saying, 'It wasn't supposed to be like this. I should never have let you go to Lanier.' Then she said, 'They threatened that if we asked any questions, they'd have to take you back.' She did tell me my name had been Cat, but she didn't seem to know any more than that, didn't want to know."

"Are you saying you were adopted?"

Diane looked at her again with that same you're-too-dense-to-live expression. "Duh."

"Did your mother give you a last name?"

"No. I wanted to know why she hadn't told me, but she kept saying she couldn't. She warned me to stay away from the clinic, not to talk to anyone and not to say another word to Johnny."

"But who set up the meeting with Hoffman?"

"Johnny. I don't know what he said to her, but she agreed to help. She promised to pass him some kind of information—"

"Only something went wrong."

"God, they killed her, like in some spy novel." She grabbed Jennifer by the shoulders, her nails digging into her skin, and stared into her face. "They killed her because of me."

"We don't know that," Jennifer soothed, prying Diane's nails off her shoulders. "Besides, the only people responsible for her death are the ones who shot her." Technically, at least.

None of this made sense. Even if Diane Robbins had been adopted, what did adoption have to do with murder, especially now, so many years later? Or with a fertility clinic?

Jennifer's heart went out to this girl, who was now slumped back against the couch looking like some street waif. She wanted to touch her, but she didn't dare. Diane had obviously spent a lot of years constructing barriers around herself, and one sob fest wasn't about to bring them down.

She wished there was something she could do to ease the girl's misery, but the plain truth was that Diane or Cat or whoever the heck she was should be talking with the police, not to Johnny Z, and certainly not to some would-be mystery writer.

"I want you to promise me you'll go straight from here to the Macon Police Department," Jennifer insisted.

The fire was back in Diane's face. "And tell them what? That I'm so screwed up that seeing the front of a doctor's office makes me crazy? No way. I hired your agency. Now *do* something! And I won't drag my mother into this. If anything were to happen to her or Dad . . . You've got to promise me, nothing will happen to my parents."

It was tempting to promise, to insist that everything was going to be fine, that it had to be some big misunderstanding. But in her heart, Jennifer was afraid Diane, as tough and self-assured as she seemed on the outside, was in the middle of something big enough to include murder. Something that would take a lot more than words to fix.

Chapter 5

"I won't get involved. I won't get involved. I won't get involved," Jennifer repeated like a mantra, punching her pillow with her fist and throwing herself hard against the bed, as if that was all it took to rid her mind of Diane Robbins.

It had taken her close to an hour and two cups of hot chocolate to get Diane's hands to stop shaking enough so she could drive herself home. There was nothing she could do to help, no matter how much she might want to. Nothing. She wasn't even a real P.I., just a tagalong, and not a very good one at that. She had done the best thing—the only thing—she could by turning the girl out.

She stared up into the darkness at her bedroom ceiling. What would it be like to go off to college, excited about a new life with new friends, and then have this kind of bombshell dropped on her? To have the entire foundation of her life, down to her name, topple out from under her?

Jennifer's own world had fallen apart when she was not all that much older than Diane. When she was a senior in college, her parents had died in a car crash. Nothing mysterious, nothing unusual. So ordinary, in fact, that it only merited a paragraph in the B section of the *Telegraph*. A few sentences to announce that Jennifer Marsh's world had changed profoundly and irrevocably.

One moment they'd been alive, loving her, being loved by her. And then they were gone.

She'd grieved until there was nothing left in her, and it hadn't made any difference. They weren't coming back, no matter how much she prayed or how desperately she thought she would die. But she had one thing that couldn't be taken from her: the absolute and complete knowledge that her parents had loved her with all their hearts. Diane didn't have that—not from her birth parents. She hadn't even known they existed. And now she was grieving for something she didn't even understand.

Jennifer rolled onto her side, propped her head up on her hand, and pushed away her memories. Johnny Zeeman. Maybe he wasn't quite the tough guy he seemed to be. He'd agreed to help Diane without a retainer. But then, maybe he'd sensed money. Lanier wasn't exactly a poor man's college. It cost every bit as much as an Ivy League school. Maybe Johnny figured her parents would come through with the cash. He'd milk it along, an adopted child's fantasy. Who knows? Maybe even a little blackmail if they were reluctant to pay.

Still, he'd contacted the nurse, and somehow persuaded her to help. Only she'd died instead, leaving a really big question: Did the nurse's death have anything to do with Diane Robbins or was it some weird coincidence?

Jennifer flung herself down on the mattress, trying again to sleep on her side, then her back, and, in desperation, upside down. Nothing seemed to work. The red numbers on her bedside clock changed with the minutes. The last ones she remembered reading were 2:57.

The sound was so soft that it barely penetrated Jennifer's sleeping brain. She stirred, wishing it away, wanting nothing more than to turn over and burrow back into the covers. But something inside her knew better and brought her suddenly and fully awake.

In the dark she could hear Muffy stir. A puff of air blew against Jennifer's cheek. The dog had planted her head on the edge of her pillow, nose-to-nose with her, eyes shining eerily. Jennifer stared at those luminescent moons as the dog drew herself up, obviously about to let out one of her major woofs.

Jennifer's mind suddenly cleared. She clamped her hand around the dog's muzzle and silently shushed her as a cold, clammy sweat broke out across her forehead and down her chest. Someone was in the living room.

The dog wiggled in her grip and started to whine. Jennifer slapped her hard on the ear, all the time holding tight to the dog's face.

Muffy looked up at her. A betrayed whimper escaped Jennifer's grip. She'd have to explain later. Right now she had an intruder to deal with and a plan to execute.

As a mystery writer, she'd thought more than once about what she might do if someone broke into her apartment. But she'd never actually expected to put it into action. And somehow she'd failed to include a greyhound in the mix.

With her free hand she dug out of the covers and swung her feet over the side of the bed. Gently she tugged Muffy to the door. It was ajar.

She could hear them now. It sounded like two men, murmuring somewhere out there. And there were muffled sounds of objects being moved, drawers being opened.

Muffy was about to burst. She struggled back and broke from Jennifer's grip, letting out a horrendous howl.

Jennifer slammed the door shut, pushed in the button on the pitiful excuse for a lock, and hit the light switch. Muffy growled and scratched at the door as Jennifer flew around the dresser and, wedging herself between it and the side wall, drew up her legs and pushed with all of her might, straining her back and cramping her legs. The dresser slid forward, against the door, just as the knob turned and rattled. Muffled curses poured from the other side, followed by a loud thump that sounded like flesh, and lots of it, hitting against the wood.

The dresser with her undies and sweaters wouldn't keep anyone out long. She dove for her mother's blanket chest that lay at the foot of the bed, tugged it sideways and rammed it with all her strength against the dresser. Then she pulled the double bed sideways, in line with both the chest and the dresser, forming a wall-to-wall barrier. The only way they'd get in now would be by beating down the upper part of the door, which, at the moment, seemed like a distinct possibility.

Muffy was hysterical, transformed into a primitive creature defending her alpha wolf and promising to eat alive anything or anyone that broke through their barrier.

Jennifer allowed herself the first full breath of air she'd taken since she heard the noise that awakened her.

But the next blow against the door put her brain back into drive and sent her scurrying for the phone. Whoever was on the other side of that door had to be armed. No one with any sense would break into a room with a raging dog unless they were.

She lifted the receiver to an open line. The vermin had taken the extension off the hook. She dropped it, flew to the window, and threw it open.

Her apartment was on the second floor above a sheer, twenty-foot drop onto grass, with a thin strip of sidewalk just to make things interesting. It wasn't so high, really, for anyone with any kind of athletic ability. To Jennifer, it seemed certain death.

She looked at the mattress. Too big. She'd never get it through the window. She grabbed the two pillows off the bed and tossed them out. They landed a good six feet apart. Then she scrambled across the bed and tore open the closet door, reaching high for the two spares she kept for company. Diving back across the bed, she tossed those out the window, too.

She heard the door splinter and grabbed Muffy, dragging her, barking and struggling, back to the window. The dog lurched against her grip, but Jennifer held her tightly against her chest as she draped one leg across the windowsill, poised to jump. They'd probably break something, most likely their heads, but she had no intention of being in that room if the door came open. Or leaving Muffy behind.

She took in a great breath of cool night air and tried to scream, but only a hoarse croak came out. Her vocal cords were knotted like fists inside her throat.

A thought flashed in her mind. She forced herself back inside, struggling against Muffy's attempts to break free, and turned on her clock radio to full volume. Then she took up her perch on the sill again and steeled herself, listening through the wail of the oldies station, waiting for the final assault on the door.

In the distance she heard sirens. Thank God for Mrs. Thorne.

Chapter 6

Short, round Mrs. Thorne shoved a cup of hot tea into Jennifer's hands. Why was it always tea? Jennifer hated tea, but she drank it anyway, grateful to have something to hold on to and something hot to soothe the shivers that skittered up her arms and down her legs.

At least she was safe. She had to be. Half of Macon's police force was standing in her apartment with a full view of her PJs. Fortunately they were her new ones, the ones with no holes in embarrassing places. And they were big, the sleeves reaching to her knuckles and the pants catching at her heels. She might not be decent, but she was covered.

She'd answered all their questions as best she could. No, she didn't know who had jimmied one lock and broken the other. No, she didn't see anything missing. No, thank God, she hadn't gotten a look at the intruders. No, it didn't make sense to her either.

Her computer, TV, answering machine, and stereo system, such as they were, were all still there. She'd flown to the closet to check her manuscripts, her most valuable possessions. They, of course, were untouched—all nine of them—valuable only to her.

Her refrigerator had been rifled through, as had every drawer, cabinet, and closet in the place. The bedroom would have been next. An entire panel had been splin-

tered in the attempt to break in the door, and then the police had been forced to break it down the rest of the way.
The dresser, the chest, and the bed were wedged so
tightly against it, there was no way she could have
moved them herself. Besides, she and Muffy seemed to
have become one with the windowsill.

The police had treated her like a jumper they were
trying to talk off a ledge. One older patrolman had lost
patience and simply pried her hands loose. It worked. To
Muffy's great relief. But now the police had lost interest
in her, apparently in agreement that she was totally use-
less in helping them. They left her alone while dusting for
fingerprints and looking for fiber evidence. Which had
left Mrs. Thorne her opening.

"Sit down, dear," Mrs. Thorne insisted, pushing Jennifer onto the couch and adjusting a pillow behind her.

She let herself be pushed, ready, for once, to let someone else be in charge. Besides, if it hadn't been for Mrs.
Thorne . . .

Muffy laid her head against Jennifer's thigh and whimpered softly. It had been a rough night for both of them.
She stroked the dog's neck.

But Jennifer was hanging in there—right up until she
spotted Sam walking through her front door.

His dark hair was a mess, his shirt open at the throat,
his sports coat rumpled. But what made her lose it was
his face: gaunt, exhausted, fearful.

She didn't know how he found out and she didn't care.
She set down her teacup and ran barefoot to him. He
hugged her tight. "Are you all right?" he whispered in
her ear.

She couldn't answer, only sob and nod vigorously
against his neck.

Sam. Thank God he had come. He cared about her,
cared that *she* was alive, not like the police, who cared

about everyone. If something happened to her, he would miss her, miss her part in his life, like she would miss him. She clung to him, ignoring how the stubble of beard on his neck scratched her face and the wool tweed of his jacket made her cheek itch. She felt safe for the first time since she'd awakened that night.

"Get your things," he ordered. "You're coming home with me."

Chapter 7

Sam's apartment was a couple of blocks off Vineville, near the historic district, on one of the city's few remaining brick streets. Unlike Atlanta, Sherman had missed Macon in his march to the sea, and the town would be forever grateful for it.

Unfortunately, Sam's appreciation of history was not matched by his housekeeping or decorating skills. While he gave lip service to the honor of living in one of these old row houses that had been divided into apartments, she secretly didn't think he deserved it. He'd lived there for over a year and still didn't have proper drapes over the windows, and he'd made no effort to furnish it.

And then there was his lifestyle. It had a tendency to interfere with neatness. Copies of *The New York Times*, *The Washington Post*, *USA Today*, and *The Philadelphia Inquirer* lay scattered across the furniture and spilled onto the floor.

Jennifer unleashed Muffy, who took a wild, panting swing through the generous living room before plopping down on the book section of the *Post*. Jennifer dragged her duffel bag out of the doorway and collapsed in the only good chair.

Sam set her computer in the corner by the makeshift brick and lumber bookshelf and headed straight to the refrigerator for a beer. He shoved the bottle in her direction between gulps, but she declined with a shake of her head. She could barely tolerate beer under any circumstances, but at seven o'clock in the morning? To be fair, it must have seemed to him like the end of a very long night.

He settled into the beanbag held together with well-placed duct tape and struggled out of his sports coat. "That didn't look like some random burglary to me," he said. "Kids do that kind of thing, the people wake up, and they're outta there. Professionals do it, they hear a dog, and they're on to the next, easier target. What's more, they didn't take anything. So what's your best guess?"

She shook her head. "I told you. I don't have one." She'd even confessed to her liaison with Johnny Z and the visit from Diane Robbins while they loaded her belongings into her Volkswagen and his Honda. She knew she shouldn't feel defensive, but she did. She didn't know what was going on. Besides, she was the victim here, and it might help if he could remember that. Victims weren't the ones with the answers. At least, not this one.

He looked to be thinking, but he wasn't about to share. He probably didn't want to scare her, which scared her even more.

Sam ran his hand through his dark, sleek hair. That was better. It looked more like she liked it—slicked back with stray strands falling over his right eye. She had to be careful about those eyes. They were the deepest, darkest blue, and when she looked too far into them . . . Well, she just needed to keep her perspective.

"Zeeman," he grunted, propping his legs on the trunk that served as a coffee table, a real trick from that angle. "How the heck did you get hooked up with that screwball? You couldn't have found a bigger nut if you'd picked him out of the phone book."

Jennifer put her hand over her throat to cover the blush she felt spreading down her neck. "Do you know him?" she asked.

"Of him. He used to be on the force, way back at the dawn of time. He and Schaeffer started out together, even partnered for a while."

So that explained the friction between the two.

"There was a question of integrity," Sam went on. "Some evidence disappeared in one of their cases, or so the story goes. No charges were brought, but Schaeffer's had it in for him ever since. He's not someone you want your name associated with. He has a way of getting into messes he should have walked away from, and now he's dragged you right into the middle of this one."

"You think Johnny Zeeman and the murdered woman have something to do with the break-in?" The thought had occurred to her, but she'd pushed it to the back of her mind. She'd had other matters to deal with, like executing her escape plan, trying to stay alive, entertaining the police, packing, and keeping Muffy off the car windows. She was hoping he'd convince her it was a ridiculous idea.

"The thought crossed my mind. What do you know about the East Lake Fertility Clinic?" he asked.

She would have preferred a simple no.

She shrugged. "I've passed by it a few times when I was in that part of town, but that's all."

He nodded and finished off the beer, letting the bottle slip to the carpet. Muffy scooted over and licked the neck. Absently, Sam batted her nose. "They keep a relatively low profile, considering the kind of business they're in."

He got up and went down the short hall to the bathroom, but soon poked his head back out, talking around a mouthful of toothbrush and toothpaste. "Feel free to take the bed. I probably won't be back until after you've gone to your writers' meeting tonight. I've got to spend most of the day covering district court, but who knows what else they'll put me on. I don't have any idea what time I'll be back, so I'll plan to eat there. If it looks like the same old, same old, I'll cut out early."

That was the worst part of his working for *The Macon Telegraph*. She never knew where he'd be when.

"And I'll see if I can't find out something about that nurse, Hoffman. What made her so special that somebody would want her dead."

He ducked back into the bathroom, and emerged with his hair combed, his face shaved, and looking only slightly worse than usual for having spent most of the early morning up with her.

As he swept past, heading for the door, she grabbed his hand. "What you said about Hoffman—you think she was killed because she was going to give Zeeman information?"

He bent down and gave her a sweet, chaste kiss, and Muffy a quick rub behind the ear. For a moment he stared at her, nose-to-nose, and she thought he was going to kiss her again. But he stood up and straightened his tie, all business.

"Don't know," he said. "Could be she was killed because somebody thought she deserved to die. That's what I intend to find out."

At the door, he stopped and turned back. "Are you going to be all right? Maybe I could get somebody to cover—"

"No, I'm fine. Don't worry."

He nodded. "There's . . . actually, there's nothing in

the refrigerator except beer and milk. But Kroger's not that far away."

She made shooing motions with her hands. She had her car and she certainly knew how to feed herself. She'd been doing it for years, and had yet to starve.

"Keep the doors locked, and don't let anybody in you don't know. And don't go back to your apartment." He looked her dead in the eye. "Promise me."

The nerve. As if she were two years old and couldn't be trusted.

She drew a cross over her heart with her index finger. "I promise."

At least for now. At least until she got the locks on her door replaced, and a solid core door installed to her bedroom with a good three-inch dead bolt. At least until she had purchased one of those chain ladders that hang outside windows. At least until she had some idea who the heck would want something they thought she had.

Chapter 8

Sam really meant it. There was *no* food in his apartment. None. She'd been through every drawer and every cabinet. All she'd found were a package of stale crackers and a left-open bag of barbecue potato chips. She'd even taken an inventory of his refrigerator: assorted out-of-date condiments and, of course, beer. Why, the man didn't even have ice cream.

And she'd had no time for shopping. She'd had to hightail it over to Dee Dee's to help put together a catering order for a birthday party that evening. She'd hoped keeping her hands busy would be a distraction from the last twenty-four hours, but Dee Dee insisted on turning on her kitchen TV while they worked.

"No no no. Absolutely not," Dr. Paul Collier told Michelle Potter, cohost of *Macon in the Morning*. "The death of Mrs. Beverly Hoffman was not related in any way to the clinic's operation. Our best guess is that she interrupted an attempted drug theft. We do, after all, have a supply of various narcotics on the premises, as does every medical facility."

"I understand Mrs. Hoffman was working late that night?"

"We don't know why Mrs. Hoffman was at the facility. We can only speculate she'd forgotten something,

38

probably of a personal nature, and had gone back to retrieve it."

"So you believe she surprised her murderers, then they panicked and shot her?"

Collier nodded his head as if he'd been there that night. Hah! What did *he* know?

"Yes. That seems to be the situation. It *was* a Sunday night. No one should have been there."

Including delivery men.

"What about the man who was in the alley that night, a private investigator by the name of Johnny Zeeman? I believe he was injured." Michelle smiled into the camera.

"I have no idea what Mr. Zeeman was doing that night, but I do know it had nothing to do with the East Lake Fertility Clinic. I can only suppose he was behind the building on some other business, surprised the hoodlums in their attempts to get away, and got himself shot in the process. It's conceivable his presence may have been the catalyst that caused the thieves to panic and kill Mrs. Hoffman."

Jennifer stopped curling carrots. Now that was a slanderous statement if she'd ever heard one. The shot that killed Hoffman was what caused her to bump the boxes and Johnny to drop his pocketknife. No way Collier was going to blame that nurse's death on them!

He looked directly into the camera. "I want to assure all of our clients and future clients that we are running at full operation and that their safety is our utmost concern. Unfortunately, drug crimes can strike anywhere, anytime."

She stared at Collier's face. Dee Dee's under-the-counter TV was not particularly kind to him. His full, salt-and-pepper beard lent an air of dignity, but he wasn't someone she'd want to entrust with her progeny, regardless of how many degrees followed his name. His

eyes were too narrow, his lips a little too fleshy, and that
twitch that tugged at the corner of his mouth a little too
suspicious. And she certainly didn't like that turtleneck
under his sports jacket, at least not on him.

She popped a carrot into her mouth. It crunched
louder than she had expected.

"I could fix you something to eat," Dee Dee offered,
not once looking up while she continued to spread the
rolled-out biscuit dough with raw sausage.

Jennifer averted her eyes. As a vegetarian, she tried to
be tolerant of the protein needs of the human species, especially those too lazy to go the bean-and-rice route and
who, instead, opted for the meat-eating easy way out.
But raw sausage on beautifully kneaded dough . . . It almost seemed like sacrilege, and quite sufficient to dull
her appetite.

"That's all right. I'm fine," she told Dee Dee, taking to
heart the tacit reprimand against eating up the food for
that night's party.

"Is he talking about that clinic you were at last night?"
Dee Dee asked ever so casually, gesturing toward the TV.

Dee Dee. So calm, so collected. She hadn't even let on
she knew what had happened when Jennifer had come to
her house to work that morning. She'd hugged her a little
tighter and longer than usual, but Jennifer thought that
was because they hadn't seen each other for a while. The
catering business was into the after-summer lull before
the fall holidays kicked off. They had three Halloween
parties scheduled, but they wouldn't be for several weeks
yet. Dee Dee had shown her the witches' costumes she
bought for them to wear, complete with little black
aprons. Oh, the joys of this business.

Tonight's shindig was a birthday party. She would
have loved to stay at Sam's that morning, but Dee Dee
really needed her help. Making carrot curls and turnip

daisies were talents not everyone possessed. And she could certainly use the money. Her meager trust fund from her parents' estate didn't do much more than cover her rent and utilities. Food was once again falling into the category of luxuries, and would most likely stay there until she finally sold a book—or the Christmas catering season started up—whichever came first.

At least she wouldn't have to serve tonight. Fortunately, it was a drop-off. She had her writers' group.

Dee Dee rolled up the dough. If only she'd substituted cinnamon, sugar, and a little butter for that sausage . . .

"I know his wife," Dee Dee said, pinching the edges of the dough together and pointing at the TV screen.

"Yeah?" That Dee Dee might know the Colliers shouldn't have surprised her. In many ways, despite its size, Macon was still a small town.

Dee Dee nodded. "She goes to church with my mother. You know how Mom's in charge of the Wednesday night suppers?"

Jennifer nodded.

"Well, the church ladies take turns helping out, and whether she's working that night or not, the whole Collier brood is there at six o'clock to eat."

"Really?" Jennifer asked casually.

"Yeah, really. Except for her husband. He never shows. I don't think he even goes to the Sunday morning service."

Dee Dee stared at Jennifer's hands. "If you rest your hands in ice water like that you'll be cracked and bleeding before morning."

Jennifer jerked her hands out and dried them. She wouldn't dare let on to Dee Dee that she might just volunteer to help at one of the Wednesday suppers. She'd never hear the end of it. But what better way to get an idea of what the clinic was like if not from the woman who was married to the director?

Dee Dee sliced another sausage twirl and laid it on the baking sheet. "So tell me," she said, looking up and smiling, "what's going on with you and Sam?"

Dee Dee had been trying to get her married for as long as they'd known each other. Dating Sam had taken some of the pressure off, but it looked like Mama Dee Dee thought now was the time for the relationship to progress.

She couldn't tell Dee Dee they were living together, even if only technically. Dee Dee would make a whole lot more out of it than was there. Worse yet, she'd have to broach what had happened at her apartment last night, a subject she had no intention of opening.

Jennifer took up a minicleaver and destroyed a bunch of broccoli florets. "Not much," she fibbed.

"You know, you really ought to decide what you want out of life, Jen."

Somehow Dee Dee had trouble separating what she herself wanted and what Dee Dee wanted *for* her.

"Wait too long and you just might be needing the services of that Dr. Paul Collier yourself someday to have Jaimie. You're born with every egg you'll ever have, you know. Every year you get older, so do they. We're not like chickens, always popping up with new ones."

Keep this up, and Jennifer could be talked into taking eggs out of her diet, too. It was at times like these that she had to remind herself how much she loved this woman.

"Mrs. Collier"—Dee Dee nodded toward the TV—"she was the reason he opened that clinic. Did you know that?" Dee Dee popped the tray of sausage twirls into the oven, set the timer for ten minutes, and rubbed her hands on her apron. "She wanted kids, and they couldn't have them the old-fashioned way."

"She told you this?"

"She tells everybody, everybody who will listen. She's got six. She's like this living, breathing advertisement for his clinic. I think she and her husband have used just about every fertility technique ever developed. As the science improved, they'd simply move onto another method. The clinic's success rate is supposed to be phenomenal. If you believe what she says, almost everyone who goes into that place comes out with a baby."

Chapter 9

Maybe, at last, Jennifer could steal a few moments for a nap before she collapsed from sleep deprivation. No one except Sam knew she'd be at his apartment, not even Dee Dee, whom she'd left with enough food to celebrate two birthdays. Of course, Dee Dee, as usual, had insisted she take some food home with her. She'd been nibbling in the car all the way over to Vineville.

As she walked across the brick parking lot toward Sam's apartment, she heard footsteps fall into rhythm behind her. She froze, bringing the rape whistle on her key ring to her lips. She drew in a lungful of air and whirled to find herself nose-to-nose with Johnny Z.

"Put that thing away, will ya?" He nodded at the whistle. "The last thing we want is to attract attention."

Startled, she let the whistle fall from her mouth and looked the man up and down. He couldn't have been much taller than her own five and a half feet. He lacked that slight droop of the eyelid, almost unnoticeable cleft of the chin, and pout of the lips, but Bogie's stare, that hint of little-boy-lost, was definitely there behind those hard features.

Johnny Z was wearing a loose cloth windbreaker that hid the bandage around his shoulder. Everything he had on looked like it'd been slept in more than once.

"What are you doing out of the hospital?" she asked.

He didn't look like he was fit to drive, let alone go visiting.

"I wanted to make sure you were all right. Schaeffer give you a hard time?"

"I can hold my own," she assured him, remembering the grin on his face when Schaeffer had hauled her out of his hospital room.

He snickered. "Helps if you don't know anything to tell. Did Robbins find you?" he asked as he furtively scanned the street and the parking lot.

"Yeah," she said, still angry he'd had the nerve to send Diane to her in the first place. "Just what the heck did you think—"

"Good. She tell you what's going on?"

"How did you find me?" she demanded.

He shrugged, wincing, the shoulder obviously still tender, and drew hard on a cigarette. Smoke curled out of his not-so-pretty mouth. "I'm paid to find people."

"Well, good for you. Go find somebody else." She turned her back on him and started toward the steps.

"This boyfriend you got, this Culpepper, you trust him?"

That stopped her cold. What kind of question was that?

"He willing to go to the mat for you?" Zeeman continued.

She could go to the mat on her own, thank you very much.

"You're not so out of the way as I'd like here," he called after her. "I'd offer you my place, but I don't suppose you'd be interested."

She turned back and gave him one of *those* looks. Besides, it wasn't like he'd be much protection in his current state.

He shrugged. "Okay. Just watch your back. It's time

you wised up, Marsh. Those people who broke into your place last night—what makes you think they can't find you as easily as I did? It's not like the boyfriend's wouldn't be the first place to look, you know."

She'd had just about all she cared to handle. Shots in alleys, late night drop-ins from strange females, uninvited visitors ransacking her apartment, overbearing friends, no food (cookies and carrots didn't count), little sleep, and seedy private eyes.

She crossed to him. "I don't need this. I'm finished. You hear me?"

He shook his head at her, an irritatingly amused smile on his lips. "You sure you're talking to the right guy? Wasn't me jimmying your lock last night." He took a final drag on the cigarette, dropped it, and stomped it out.

"That's littering," she informed him.

"So you want none of it, huh? Maybe you can send the guys who dropped by your place last night a little note to that effect, just so they don't come back and inconvenience you."

"Fine. You tell me who *they* are, and I'll do just that."

"Ain't that easy, doll. That's the part we gotta work on. What I'm worried about right now is what we do between the here and the there, the time when they know who we are and we figure out who they are."

Jennifer was becoming sorrier by the minute that she'd ever pulled out those yellow pages.

He leaned closer and lowered his voice. She could smell the smoke on his breath. "There're things you need to know."

"So clue me in," she demanded.

He stopped her cold with his stare. "I think you'd better come with me," he told her. "Talking out here ain't such a good idea."

"But I—" she started, and then stopped. Clearly, Johnny wasn't going to take no for an answer. And what the heck! What she did or did not want seemed irrelevant. Somehow or other, she'd unwittingly become entangled with Diane Robbins and Johnny Zeeman in a way that required more than walking away to undo.

"Okay," she said, "but I have to be back before too late. I have group tonight."

"What's that? A therapy session?"

"It might as well be."

Chapter 10

Johnny's office was an upstairs hole-in-the-wall with his name printed on the window overhanging the street à la Sam Spade. Bleak, unkempt, and musty. She didn't even know they had places like that in Macon. To make the scene complete, all Johnny needed were spastic neon lights flashing through the dingy glass and a fifth of whiskey in the desk drawer.

He ushered her over to a metal chair with a padded vinyl seat. She swatted at it with a tissue from her purse and sat down. Johnny leaned back against his desk and gave her a good once-over.

"Okay, I'm here. So what was so important that you couldn't tell me in the parking lot?" she demanded.

She hoped she hadn't made a big mistake coming up here with him. But surely he was too weak to try anything, even if the thought crossed his mind.

"You know, Marsh, people who face death together develop a certain bond. . . ."

She rolled her eyes. "Don't even go there."

He shifted and crossed his ankles. "Robbins tell you about coming across the clinic and having an episode of déjà vu?" he asked.

How about that? He knew French. "Yep."

He twisted, picked up a folder off the desk, and tossed it into her lap.

"What's this?"

"Most of what there is to know about the East Lake Fertility Clinic."

She looked at him quizzically. "But I thought you told Schaeffer you didn't know anything about the clinic."

"Did I say that? Must have been a misunderstanding. I thought he asked me what I was doing in the alley. You really think I'd go into a job without having checked the place out? I'm disappointed in you, Marsh."

Now it was her turn to be angry. "You took me into that situation knowing it was dangerous, knowing—"

"Hey hey hey! Don't go getting your tail all in a knot. There was no reason for me or Diane to think meeting Hoffman was going to go down like it did. It should have been a simple hand-off."

"A hand-off of what?"

"I don't know, honest."

Yeah, like she was going to believe him! She shook her finger at him. "You led Schaeffer to believe Diane was the one who had been killed."

He grunted. "Don't kid yourself. Schaeffer knew who the victim was before he walked into my hospital room." He straightened and shifted. The shoulder must have been kicking up. "Besides, I never saw the woman who was killed. Remember? You did."

He was doing it again, making her feel as though she'd somehow been dishonest.

"The clinic's been in operation close to twenty-five years," he continued. "The head honcho is one Paul Collier."

"I saw him on *Macon in the Morning*."

Zeeman pursed his lips, dug in his pocket and came up with a cigarette. "So he's already at it, putting his spin on things. Any of the rest of them show up with him?"

He lifted the cigarette in her direction, but she shook her head. "The rest?" she asked.

Johnny struck a match, put it to the cigarette, and drew hard as the fire worked itself into the tobacco. He let out a mouthful of smoke.

Boy, he did like his nicotine. She could almost see the wave of calm spread through his body.

"The other partners are his brother Donald and Doctors McEvoy and Sullivan. The story goes that Collier—Paul—and wife were looking to start a family but with little success. They came upon McEvoy, who, with Sullivan, had perfected a procedure that was resulting in a good rate of pregnancies among infertile couples. They tried it, it worked for them. So they lured the doctor duo away from some facility up north to Macon with promises of wealth and the relative comfort of Southern life."

"Is the success rate at the clinic really that impressive?"

"Apparently. My guess is they keep their numbers up through good screening. They only take on clients they're pretty certain they can help."

"Sounds admirable. And brother Donald?"

"He came along about eleven years after the clinic opened, after his stint through med school, residency, and a partnership in some fertility clinic somewhere along the mid-Atlantic. Some questions arose over his screening procedures after the deaths of a couple who were under his care—"

"Deaths? Good grief! What'd he do to them?"

Johnny shook his head. "Nothin' like that. Some kind of domestic dispute between the husband and wife."

"Then why—"

"The feeling was he shouldn't be helping people who were unstable bring babies into this world."

"Was he sued?"

"No, but you shake the public's confidence in a business like that, and you don't have no business. He went looking for more fertile ground."

She groaned. Cutesy didn't go with Johnny. He couldn't quite pull it off. "So what's all this got to do with anything?"

"Just giving you the lay of the land."

"Why'd you ask me up here, Johnny?"

He stared at her a moment longer than he should have, and she blushed.

"Marsh," he said quietly, lighting another cigarette from the one in his mouth. "I didn't come get you for your help. I came because I feel responsible for getting you involved. I should never have taken you with me that night."

She nodded. It was an apology of sorts, and somehow made her feel a little less used.

He drew long and hard on the fire. "Those thugs who broke into your place think you have whatever it was that nurse was going to hand over to us in the alley. They know I don't have it. Ten to one they searched my things at the hospital while I was getting patched up."

"But how could they—" she started.

He blew smoke out his nostrils. "*You* got in, didn't you?"

She sank back into her chair like a deflating balloon. "But they wouldn't know my—"

"That little appearance you made on TV, even if you didn't say anything. Always better to keep a low profile. Stay away from cameras. You get a person's face, you can find out who they are."

She sat stunned, her heart beating almost as fast as it had in the alley. All along she'd felt there was a connection between what had happened in the alley and the break-in at her apartment, but she'd tried to shrug it off, tried to pretend it was all over with, that whoever had done it was satisfied and gone. Only Johnny wouldn't let her. He thought she was still in danger, and he wasn't about to let her forget it.

"You better stick with me, see this through," he told her. "I'd hate to see anything happen to you."

He wasn't the only one.

He reached into a side drawer of the desk, and she half expected him to pull out a fifth of bourbon. Instead he came up with a small pistol. "I'd feel better if you kept this with you for a while." He offered her the gun.

She stared at it. Her fictional detective Maxie Malone carried a gun; so did Jolene Arizona, a character she'd prefer to forget she ever created. Still, for Jennifer, guns inspired terror, almost as much terror as the people who carried them. They were too loud, too deadly. She shoved it back toward Johnny Z. "No thanks. I'll take my chances."

She licked her lips. Seeing the gun had brought it all home to her. No more pretending. She'd really done it this time. Like it or not, whatever was going on, it was dangerous, and she was right in the middle of it.

"So what do we do next?" Jennifer asked.

"You? Nothin'. Stay low. Write your little books. I'm going to do some more snooping around this clinic. The nurse promises to give me some information; she winds up dead. Stands to reason it's because of someone she told or someone who seen what she was up to."

Maybe Johnny was more competent than his reputation would suggest. He had, after all, dragged himself out of that hospital bed even if the clause in Diane's contract would have allowed him to continue to collect his fee while he healed. Assuming he ever collected a fee. As long as he was watching out after Diane, she ought to be all right.

And maybe, if she told herself that often enough, she might even begin to believe it.

Chapter 11

"Nice of you to call back," Teri chided. Her perfectly plucked eyebrows arched above her half-lidded eyes, lending her cocoa face an exotic air. Her lean, athletic body was hidden beneath a huge T-shirt and baggy shorts. She sat in a lotus position, with her back leaning against Monique's sofa, her palms resting upright on her knees, chanting *ohms*.

Jennifer, still rattled from her session with Johnny Z, stepped over Teri and pointed out, "If you were doing that right, you wouldn't even notice I was here."

She settled next to Leigh Ann on part of the sectional. She'd come to her weekly writers' meeting in hopes that, for at least two hours, she could lose herself in her secure world of writing and forget all about threats and untimely death—except fictional ones, of course.

"Now, you be nice," petite, green-eyed Leigh Ann chastised Teri, who gave up all pretense at meditation to glare back at her.

Leigh Ann reminded Jennifer of a china doll, with her ivory skin and dark hair, but only in looks. There was nothing fragile about Leigh Ann.

"Our Jen's been through a lot," Leigh Ann went on, patting Jennifer on the knee. "She was shot at, you know, and that's not to be taken lightly. We could just as easily be meeting at the funeral home right now." Her gaze drifted wistfully toward the ceiling, and it seemed as though she were having a vision. "Poor Jennifer. Cut flowers and wreaths everywhere, lightly scenting the air, candles creating a halo effect against burgundy velvet drapes in some dim little parlor. The four of us, our bodies wracked with sobs, passing tissues back and forth, all wondering what Sam was going to do without our dear Jennifer and who he was going to do it with. And Jen, herself, tucked snugly in the pink satin of a dark mahogany—"

"Pink?" Teri interrupted. "Blue, maybe—"

"I was thinking lilac," April threw in.

Monique, firmly planted in her rocking chair, loudly cleared her throat, and both Teri and Leigh Ann looked up, startled, as if they'd been caught doing something they shouldn't, which as far as Jennifer was concerned, they had. Monique was fortyish, just enough older to inspire some respect. But it was the fact that she had a real-life published book to her credit that made her the undisputed leader of the group. When she spoke, they didn't.

April shifted on the opposite couch, her long blond curls framing her sweet, round face. She looked ready to pop, more pregnant than Jennifer had ever seen anybody ever. And she'd watched April, week by week, grow through her first pregnancy to produce a nine-pound baby boy. This one promised to be even bigger, as April munched on a piece of peanut-butter-stuffed celery, one of her favorite and more healthy snacks.

"I brought some peanut butter muffins, too, one for everybody," she offered, obviously hoping to break the tension.

Last week's peanut butter pie had been truly unique. Looked like month nine had a theme.

"How about you, Jennifer? You probably need some protein after last night." April held the Baggie in her direction.

Jennifer shook her head. She didn't need anything sticking to the roof of her mouth. She had enough stuck in her craw.

"So, you going to tell us about it?" Teri fixed her again with her dark eyes.

"Okay." Jennifer sighed. She had to say something. They'd never leave her alone until she did. At least the break-in at her apartment was so unnewsworthy it wouldn't be mentioned in the newspaper. "I was doing research—for my new Serena Callas mystery."

Teri clucked her tongue. "The girl never learns. Haven't you heard of the library?"

"Don't interrupt. I want to hear this." Leigh Ann leaned forward.

"Shots were fired, someone got killed, and I just happened to be there. That's all I'm going to say, and I'd appreciate it if you wouldn't discuss my death, at least not in my presence, that is, while I'm still alive. Not that I plan to die anytime soon . . ."

They all turned to her as if she were crazy and the one who had brought up the subject in the first place.

"You left out one little detail—Johnny Zeeman was shot," Teri said. "Not cool. You two were in that alley alone together." She raised one eyebrow at Jennifer. "You got something going with him?"

Now this was a direction she hadn't expected, but she should have. Teri wrote romantic suspense. As far as she was concerned, danger and romance were one word. But Jennifer and Johnny Z? An involuntary shudder shook her shoulders. "Teri . . ." she warned.

Teri shrugged. "Had to ask."

"Oh, Johnny's not so bad," Leigh Ann threw in.

Now it was Leigh Ann's turn to be stared at. Of course. Johnny was single. Jennifer had long suspected Leigh Ann knew every available man in Macon. Now she was sure of it.

"What?" Leigh Ann asked defensively.

A picture was forming in Jennifer's mind, and it wasn't pretty. "Jeez, Leigh Ann. Please don't tell me you dated him?"

"Only once. He kind of reminded me of someone, but I never figured out who it was."

Yeah, Humphrey Bogart. But only Bogie could pull off looking like that and make it sexy.

Fortunately Monique felt moved to speak. Whatever else an__ __ __ __ __ ___ay about Monique's reign of terror, it __ __ __ __ __ __ r on occasion, especially when they __ __ __ __ __ ke Leigh Ann's love life.

__ __ __ __ __ thing this past week?" It was the __ __ __ __ __ e weekly rejection update. It sent __ __ __ __ __ tter every time she heard it, with __ __ __ __ read.

__ __ __ ipts or at least query letters out __ __ __ __ __t's or editor's desk. Once again __ __ __ __ __ out the first three chapters of Maxie __ __ __e's second adventure, the one she'd come so close to selling, the one for which two editors had actually asked to see the whole manuscript. It had promise; they both said so. So why wouldn't one of them just *buy* it?

It'd been gone a good three months this time, a fact that could be very good or very bad. If it were good, that meant some editorial assistant had probably read it, liked it, and bumped it up to an editor before making the request for the rest of it. If it were bad, it meant her chapters were probably languishing in the great black hole known as the unsoliciteds. Over the holidays, some minimum-wage college student would most likely clear out the stack, stuffing them back into their self-addressed-stamped envelopes. They made such nice Christmas presents.

April cleared her throat. "Remember my series proposal about Billy and his sidekick, Barney, the Flying Squirrel?"

How could she forget? She was the one who'd suggested that April change Barney from a bat with possibly rabid tendencies to a squirrel, and that she make Billy older, eight rather than four. Early readers would surely respond better to simple mysteries than the picture book group.

"Well, it may be nothing, but I have some interest in it. They liked the proposal and want to see the first book, *The Case of the Missing Nuts.*"

"That's wonderful," Jennifer blurted out, a stupid-looking smile frozen on her face. Half of her was truly and unconditionally excited for April, but she couldn't deny the pang of unwanted, low-down, mean, unjustified jealousy that swept through her. What a wretched creature she was. She wished, however briefly, that she could be the one saying those words. Of course, not about the squirrel book. She didn't want to write about nuts.

"Excellent," Monique was saying. "Let us know the minute you hear anything."

Jennifer suspected somewhere under that beam of approval lay another jealous heart.

Monique went straight to the night's business. "I believe Teri has something she wants to discuss. Go ahead."

"Yeah. I need some help brainstorming. I'm starting a new book."

"Another romantic suspense?" Monique asked.

What else?

Teri nodded. "I thought I'd do something with a baby in it."

Leigh Ann nodded. "An old tried and true."

April looked a little confused.

"Oh, you know the list of favorite romance plots," Leigh Ann explained. "Marriage of convenience, lost love, weddings, amnesia, second chance, Cinderella, Beauty and the Beast, anything with a cowboy. Were you thinking of a variation on secret baby?"

"Something like that," Teri agreed. "I'm thinking she's in her mid-twenties, a successful career woman who's sublimated her sexuality to the point of sainthood. Her one true love, her college sweetheart, split when he found out she was pregnant, and—"

"This is your hero?" Leigh Ann broke in. "A deserter?"

"You can't have a secret baby without a father, at least not any way I've figured out," Teri insisted. "Besides, he's been in the service—a Navy SEAL—"

"They are so cool," Leigh Ann interrupted. "And those wet suits . . ." She licked her lips.

Teri rolled her eyes. "Anyway, he's been out at sea on some kind of three-year tour—"

"They never keep them out longer than six months or so," Leigh Ann corrected her.

No one argued with Leigh Ann about servicemen.

"Okay. I'll work that out later. But he hasn't gone one day without thinking of her and their child. He's got his head on straight, and he's come back to claim them as soon as he can."

"Okay, but where's the conflict?" Jennifer asked. "Not that I know much about romance." She had to get that in before one of them pointed it out to her. "But it seems to me you could write this one as a short story."

Teri looked at her through half-lidded eyes. "It's emotional, Jennifer. She has to forgive him, learn to trust again."

"Fine. But I don't see how you can write three hundred pages about it," Jennifer insisted, crossing her arms.

"Excuse me," April said. "What about the baby?"

"The baby's a device," Teri said. "You know, like the children you see on soap operas."

"Yeah," Leigh Ann said, tossing her hair. "When I have a child, I want one like that. No diapers, no midnight feedings. They're always at the park with Grandma or the nanny. Then they disappear and come back all grown up."

Sort of like Diane.

"That's not right." April shifted again, a living, breathing example of what motherhood was really all about. "Children are people, too, you know."

Monique leaned forward. "We need more. You can't go on chapter after chapter with him waiting patiently while she resolves her feelings for him. He's got to be in conflict, too."

Teri knitted her brow. "Okay, then. It hasn't been too long since baby switches were all over the news. What if the child she's been raising is not really their baby? What if it was swapped and neither one of them knows it? They have to discover together what happened to their child."

What happened to their child. The words echoed in Jennifer's ears.

But Jennifer didn't have long to think. April had

shifted into crisis mode. Her eyes were huge, her face red, and she'd started rapidly blowing little puffs of air. Jennifer had seen something like that once on PBS before she'd been able to find the remote and switch the channel. Something akin to panic was attacking her gut. If Teri sent April into labor . . .

"You all right?" Jennifer soothed.

April shook her head between puffs. "I can't listen to this." She stuck her fingers in her ears and started lalaing loudly.

Jennifer jabbed Teri. "Are you crazy? You can't start talking about baby switches around a woman who's about to go into labor. What if she refuses to go to the hospital, and we have to deliver the baby right here?" She jabbed Teri again.

"Sorry, Miss Scarlett, but I don't know nothin' 'bout birthin' babies. Looks like you'll have to do it yourself."

She folded her arms and leaned back against the sofa, refusing any responsibility for the crisis she'd started.

Monique glowered, using the same death stare her main character employed in *Double Sun, Double Trouble*. Fortunately, none of them keeled over. She reached over and pulled April's fingers out of her ears. "Stop that," she ordered.

April stopped but her face remained red. She picked up some manuscript pages, rapidly fanned herself, and swallowed hard. "I'm fine. Really. But I want to go home."

It took the three of them—Leigh Ann's featherweight didn't count—to get April up.

She was truly shaken, and she had every right to be. When a woman gives birth, she shouldn't have to worry about whether the baby she takes home is her own.

And the baby?

The baby shouldn't have to worry about who she is and what happened to her real parents.

Chapter 12

Jennifer spent the drive from Monique's house to Sam's apartment staring into the darkness and wondering how she'd wound up in the eighth ring of Dante's Hell, the one reserved for singles trying to define their relationships.

She *had* to talk to Sam if they were going to share an apartment for even a short time. There was only one bed, one bedroom, and no real couch, which meant sleeping arrangements, at the very least, promised to be interesting.

She'd successfully kept their relationship in limbo for months, a fine dance of denial. She hadn't been looking for anything when Sam dropped into her life. Actually, she'd been actively avoiding it, but he'd charmed her with his unjaded, almost naive belief in his work, and with his understanding of her dream to become a published author. He'd seen her vision and he hadn't laughed. He'd admired her for it and paid her the highest compliment someone can pay an aspiring writer: he believed she could do it.

Of course, it didn't hurt that he was cute, could be most endearing when he wasn't actively irritating her, and had a way of seeing straight into her soul. A mixed blessing. She was afraid she'd fall in love with him before she was ready.

This morning she'd been too confused, too worried, too scared to consider the implications of staying at Sam's. Now they were flashing at her like yellow warning lights around a BRIDGE OUT sign. And she saw no way to turn back. If she went over the edge . . .

She could hear him fussing in the kitchen as she let herself in the front door.

"That you?" he called out.

"Yeah," she answered. "Where's Muffy?"

"She's having ice cream in the bathroom."

He'd put up the dog. And gone to the grocery, at least to get ice cream, a necessary staple of her life.

She glanced around the living room. He'd picked up. He must have been having the same conversation with himself that she'd been having on the way over, only she spied evidence that he'd already come to a conclusion.

A single red rose stood in a vase next to a liter of ginger ale and four glasses.

Her head snapped back. Four?

Diane poked her nose out of the kitchen nook. "Sam says you like the mild salsa." She wrinkled her nose.

Jennifer nodded automatically, and Diane disappeared back around the corner. Had she missed something? What the heck was Diane Robbins doing at Sam's apartment? She thought she'd made it clear last night she had nothing to offer the girl. And besides, how did Diane know where to find her?

She dumped her briefcase next to the door.

Sam brought in a bowl of chips. Diane followed, carrying the dish of salsa and licking her fingers. A second young woman, with shoulder-length, naturally, orange-red hair, and a fresh freckled face, was right behind with a stack of napkins. What the heck was all this about?

The girls—Diane in her black turtleneck, the other girl

in a Lanier College sweatshirt—settled on the floor around the food atop the trunk that served as a coffee table and began munching loudly.

Jennifer cleared her throat.

"Oh, yeah," Diane said. "Jennifer Marsh, this is Valerie Wolfe, my roommate."

The girl, small-boned and delicate, stuffed a chip into her mouth, brushed the salt from her fingers, and offered a shy smile along with her hand. Jennifer took it, too polite not to.

"Nice to meet you, Valerie."

Valerie closed her eyes and held on tight.

"Don't mind her," Diane said, nodding at Valerie. "She's into vibes, tarot, channeling—all that esoteric stuff. She's reading you."

Jennifer jerked her hand back, and Valerie's eyes snapped open. She was flushed.

"Wow!" she said. "When were you born? You must be a fire sign."

Jennifer sent a look of panic in Sam's direction. He flashed one of his super smiles, the one that was a little too good to be real. "How about that. Forgot the ice. Jen, you want to give me a hand?"

Somehow she wasn't at all sure going into another room with Sam was the best idea. If he were going to do her damage, she wanted witnesses, even if they were Wednesday and Tabitha.

He cornered her next to the refrigerator. "I thought I made it clear I didn't want you associating with Zeeman. Why the heck did you tell him he could send them over here?"

"Me? I didn't. And who are you to tell me what to do? I'll associate with whomever I please whether I want to or not. Besides, you're the one who let them in."

"Oh, no no no. You don't get off that easy. Diane

belongs to you," he reminded her. "And apparently Valerie belongs to Diane."

Great. She was beginning to feel like a set of nesting dolls, afraid to unscrew the next one to see who came out, and definitely not fond of the idea of anybody belonging to her.

"If you think I had anything to do with this . . ." She shook her head and then realized her mistake. She'd forgotten the cardinal rule: when attacked, never fall into a defensive posture.

"You fixed snacks," she countered. "What were you thinking? You don't get rid of unwanted company by feeding them."

"They were hungry. What was I supposed to do?"

Worked every time.

"I don't know, but you don't offer them chips. What's the story? They must have told you something to get you to let them in."

He was a softie, even if he wouldn't admit it.

"Diane said Zeeman gave her the address because he has no secretary to put them up and was afraid of the legal implications if he let them stay with him. They're both seventeen."

Stay? No wonder he was so upset. "Why would they need a place—"

"Their dorm room was tossed. Apparently Valerie freaked out when she found it. Said it 'reeked of evil.' The lock is being changed but neither one of them will go back."

"Their dorm room?" Wasn't anyplace safe? "When?"

"Late last night. Valerie says she was studying at the library, and, from what Diane can figure, she must have been at your place. When she got home, she found Valerie hysterical and the place upside down. They went to their residence director, who called the police and instituted extra security. But they're having none of it."

"Didn't anybody see anything?"

"Apparently not. The police asked around, but no one on the floor noticed any strangers. Valerie said she found the mess when she got back from the library. The two of them spent the rest of the night and most of the morning filling out paperwork. They made it over to IHOP for lunch, where they tried to figure out what to do next. They were afraid somebody might be watching Valerie's car, so they hitched a ride to Johnny's office. He wasn't there. They had to wait until he got back. After some discussion, he left them off over here."

"I see. So I'm supposed to—"

"Play den mother, I guess." Sam grinned at her, obviously pleased that if he had to be inconvenienced, she would be, too. "Unless you have a better idea."

She didn't, but she would have given a lot for one. Herding teenagers made her feel old, and she was still solidly in her twenties—at least for another six months. What's more, she'd already said everything she had to say to Diane.

"This is hardly what I'd planned for tonight," he told her, softening, at least a little.

"I know," she said, tugging at the front of his shirt.

He searched her eyes, and she couldn't help but wonder what he would have said if they had been alone. Then he pulled her close, his breath in her ear. It felt so right, so—

"We need something to drink in here," Diane called from the other room.

They broke apart, like two teenagers caught doing something they shouldn't.

He turned and opened the freezer, pulling out two trays of ice that he cracked into a mixing bowl.

"How was court?" she asked.

"The usual. Mostly DUIs, nothing exciting."

"This morning on *Macon in the Morning*, Collier said the guys that shot Hoffman were after drugs. What do you think of that possibility?"

He handed her the bowl, along with a pair of tongs. "I think if I were going to break into a doctor's office looking for drugs, I wouldn't pick a fertility clinic. And I know I wouldn't bother to bring a van and deck myself out in a uniform."

"Maybe not you, but—"

"Don't ask for my opinion if you don't want it, Jen. I won't lie to you just to make you feel better."

She knew that. Sam's honesty was one thing she could count on. She'd just hoped that maybe they could all chalk Hoffman's murder up to another drug theft gone bad.

They exchanged one last look. Then she followed Sam into the living room, where she filled the glasses with ice and added the ginger ale.

Valerie stared up at her from under her eyelashes with a kind of awe. "Johnny said you write mysteries as well as being a P.I. He thinks you're real cool."

Sam raised an eyebrow at Jennifer, and she blushed.

"You ever put your real cases into your books?" Valerie continued.

She opened her mouth to explain that Johnny was not exactly telling the truth, but Diane jumped in, crunching loudly on a chip. "She won't admit to anything," she said, nailing Jennifer with her stare, "but I think I've got it all figured out. She's kind of like those old-fashioned, hard-boiled writers who get involved with real-life murders, solve them, keep a low profile, let the police take the credit. So don't ask her. She'll only deny it."

"Golly. I've never met a real-life Jessica Fletcher before." Valerie seemed definitely awestruck, and Sam was having far more fun with this than he should.

Diane rolled her eyes.

Jennifer didn't bother to point out that Jessica Fletcher was hardly hard-boiled. *And* fictional. And that any association with her was dangerous. The death rate for people even marginally acquainted with her was far higher than the national average. By now the population of Cabot Cove, Maine, had to have been reduced to a mere shell of its former self. Still, she wouldn't mind having Jessica around. In one hour they'd all know whodunit. As it stood now, she was still trying to figure out what was done.

"I'm not—" Jennifer began.

"See? I told you. All she'll do is deny it," Diane repeated.

"Might as well tell them the truth," Sam said, his eyes grinning while his mouth didn't dare. "She's really pretty good at the figuring-out part. It's the doing part—"

Jennifer nudged him, and he intelligently shut up.

"So where do we go from here?" Diane asked. "What's the plan?"

The plan? Jennifer sighed and settled into the only good chair. She had two girls who evidently had no intention of leaving her side until all this was over, one murder, two men who wanted whatever that nurse had planned to pass to Johnny, and one questionable P.I. Fortunately, Johnny seemed to have the clinic covered. That left Diane's past.

"Where you from?" Jennifer asked.

"Smith Mountain."

"Never heard of it."

"Like who has? It's about as far north and east as you can go and still be in Georgia, way up near the borders with Tennessee and North Carolina."

"What's your dad do up there?"

"He's a consultant. Travels a lot."

"How long has he been doing that?"

"Long as I can remember."

"And your mom?"

"Nothin'. She elevated staying home with me to an art."

Not exactly nothing in Jennifer's opinion, but definitely interesting. Either this family loved mountain air or they had taken pains to keep themselves isolated.

"Tell me again what your mother told you."

"She said I was adopted."

"And you didn't know it?"

Diane shook her head.

Bummer. It was hard enough to deal with finding out something like that without having death and mayhem a part of it.

"And for some reason you think your adoption is connected to the clinic?"

Diane nodded. "I remember the place. I get all goose-bumpy even thinking about it. And my mom freaked when I mentioned it." She shuddered.

"Really bad vibes," Valerie said. "The place is, like, evil."

It was always good to have an impartial viewpoint.

"If you remember the clinic, you weren't an infant," Sam said.

"Try three. At least Mom told me that much."

"I can't imagine a clinic being legally involved in an adoption," Sam commented. "I'd say the first thing to do is find a record of the adoption."

"Sounds pretty straightforward. Can you do that for us?" Jennifer asked him.

"Sure. If Diane will give me the complete names of her

parents and their Social Security numbers, if she knows them, I'll check it out first thing in the morning."

She nodded. "And I'd say the second thing to do is to have a face-to-face with your parents. How long will it take us to get there?"

"Three hours, maybe a little more."

"Good. Let's get some rest. We're headin' out in the morning." Jennifer stood up.

Diane shook her head vigorously.

"What?" Jennifer asked impatiently.

"Dad's on a business trip, and Mom's not there."

"What do you mean?"

"I tried to call several times after what happened at the clinic. No answer. I finally got hold of a neighbor. Mom left early yesterday morning. Nobody knows where she is."

Sam threw Jennifer a look, and she let out a deep sigh. Add one missing person to the list. She didn't like the way things were tallying up.

"Okay. Then it will have to be the clinic." She knew Johnny could only do so much there. "We'll have to devise some kind of plan to get someone inside. We'll start tomorrow, so you'd better get some sleep."

"But—" Diane began.

"Look, you wanted a plan, so you'll just have to go with it."

"But—" she repeated.

Jennifer shook her head. "We either do this or we—"

"She wants to know where we're going to sleep," Valerie said. "We checked out the place. Only one bed."

"Not to worry," Sam said, getting up and ducking into the bedroom. He came back dragging two sleeping bags and an air mattress, which he dumped in a heap in the middle of the floor.

"Got another one of those things?" Jennifer asked, pointing at one of the rolls.

"You sure—"

"I'm sure." She was not a happy camper. She was way too tired to consider addressing their relationship in the middle of murder and in front of witnesses. Besides, she didn't particularly trust herself. She didn't want to say or do anything she might regret later. There must be something to that danger and sex combination that Teri was always writing about.

"I can put together a bedroll made of blankets, if that will do," he told her.

"That will be just fine."

"Okay, but I really thought—"

"Sometimes you think too much," she said, unrolling a bag.

"I guess you're right. I just thought maybe you'd be more comfortable in the bed, especially since you didn't get much sleep last night. But I guess I don't really need to sleep next to the door. Muffy will be in here, and she'll let us know if anyone tries anything."

She looked up at him and rued the hardness of the floor. When would she ever learn to let someone finish a whole sentence?

Chapter 13

"Remember that book you were working on a few months back where your heroine was kept against her will at that mental institution?" Jennifer asked, trying to untwist the phone cord that insisted on bunching into a mass of curls atop Sam's nightstand.

She had slipped out of the living room, stepping over the sleeping bodies of Diane and Valerie, and taken refuge in the bedroom. Muffy had come along, apparently to make sure she stayed out of trouble.

Sam was long gone to work. He must have been really quiet getting ready because all she remembered hearing was the refrigerator door opening and Muffy whimpering. Then something touched her cheek, but by the time she managed to pry her eyes open, the door was closing behind him.

When she'd stirred again, it was after eight-thirty. She wanted to catch Teri before nine o'clock while she was still in her semicomatose, I-can't-believe-I'm-at-work-this-early-in-the-morning state, which seemed to persist at least until her second cup of office coffee.

"You called me to ask about a plot I threw out three months ago? I *am* trying to work here. Like to tell me what's up?"

She was grateful that photo phones were still a thing

of the future. Teri could nail her in a moment face-to-face, and, unfortunately, she seemed unusually alert this morning.

"I was working on something, and I thought maybe it would help if—"

"Ever heard of plagiarism? Don't you go stealing any of my ideas," Teri warned. "I hardly have enough for myself."

"Teri!" Jennifer had had about all of this she could handle. All she'd done was ask a simple question. "Either tell me or—"

"Okay, sure. It's not like I'm ever going to finish that book anyway. I really liked it, but after the hero broke her out, I never could come up with a plausible reason for her being there in the first place. It didn't help that I'd made her mute. If the woman had simply talked to me—"

Only to a writer could that make any sense.

"Remind me how you got him undercover in the clinic."

"Oh, so that's what you're after. Simple. I signed him up as an orderly."

Darn.

"But what would you have done if it had been a smaller operation? What if—"

"Okay, spill it," Teri ordered. "If I'm going to be using company time for personal matters, I want to know what the matter is."

"Spill what?" Jennifer asked innocently.

"You're messin' in something you shouldn't be again."

"I don't know what—"

"Jen, cut the crap and fess up. If you didn't need my help, you wouldn't have called me."

She winced. It was truth time. "I've kind of inherited Johnny Z's client."

"Just how do you *inherit* a client? Did he die or somethin'?"

"She's only seventeen. It's not like I can just leave her to trust—"

"Okay. You've lost me completely."

Jennifer settled onto the side of the bed, and Muffy grabbed the phone cord in her mouth. Jennifer pried it loose, and the dog let out an indignant woof before lying down on top of her feet. If she wasn't going to be any fun, Muffy would make sure she couldn't move. Jennifer let out an exasperated grrrrr.

"So now you're growling at me?" Teri said.

"No. Look. All you need to know is that I need a way to get some information from the East Lake Fertility Clinic. They don't have orderlies, and I certainly can't wait for someone to get a job there. Any suggestions?"

The pause on the other end of the line was ominous.

"Exactly what kind of information?"

"My best guess is that Johnny's client, Diane Robbins, was adopted through the clinic about fourteen years ago."

She heard a gasp over the line.

"Are we talkin' baby-selling here? Because I've never heard of a fertility clinic being involved with adoptions. Kind of defeats the whole purpose, don't you think? Cuts into their profit margin."

"Or adds to it," Jennifer pointed out, rubbing Muffy's head, which was now firmly planted on her knees. "I'm afraid that's exactly what we may be dealing with. Whoever shot that nurse already knows who I am."

"And how do you know that?" Teri asked.

Jennifer explained, in the barest of terms, about the break-in at her apartment.

"Jeez, child. What have you gone and gotten yourself into?"

Teri didn't rattle easily, and to hear the concern in her voice created an empty feeling in Jennifer's stomach. "Look, maybe I could—"

"Saw this on a soap opera once—actually more than once. Some woman pretends to be pregnant. Gets away with it for a whole nine months. Maybe one of us could offer up some 'merchandise' for the baby peddlers. How hard could it be for one visit?"

"Impossible—that's how hard. Teri, don't do anything foolish."

Jennifer had known better than to call Teri, but who else was there?

"Don't have a hissy fit. I was just thinking out loud. Let me get this straight so you won't yell at me later. What you want to know is—"

"Is the clinic involved with adoptions—legal or illegal? I thought maybe somebody could drop by and simply ask if adoption was something the clinic could help with."

"Not to worry. Consider it covered."

"Teri, all I wanted were some ideas—"

"I tell you, we'll handle it."

" 'We'? You couldn't possibly be thinking of calling Leigh Ann. . . ."

"Leigh Ann? You've got to be kidding. That girl is nothin' but trouble. Besides, how could she help me get inside a fertility clinic? She's way too young."

"But—"

"Chill, babe. Talk to you soon."

The phone buzzed in her ear as terror settled in her bones and Muffy stared up at her. Someday she'd figure out that doing nothing might be less productive but a whole lot less terrifying than getting Teri involved.

Chapter 14

Jennifer drummed her fingers on the small table at the new age coffee shop/bookstore down the street from the *Telegraph* offices and took another sip of water. Sam was late, as usual, and her stomach was doing double loops waiting to be fed.

He swept in looking attractively disheveled, spied her in the back, and came grinning toward her, obviously pleased with himself.

"It's harder to find something that's not there than something that is," he declared, loosening his tie and settling into one of the flimsy wooden chairs.

The waitress was right on top of them. Jennifer ordered a vegetarian delight and a cappuccino. They made some of the best specialty coffees in Macon.

Sam requested a meatball sub and a plain coffee—assuming someone in the place knew how to brew one.

When the waitress was out of earshot, Sam leaned forward and filled her in. "Diane Robbins was not legally adopted in the state of Georgia by Stewart G. and Anne Marie Robbins, nor was any other child by any other name."

"You're sure?" Jennifer asked, not at all ready to accept what he was saying. "What about variations in name spelling?"

"Absolutely sure. I also looked for S-t-u-a-r-t, A-n-n,

even Mary. Tried with the initials and without. Nothing—five years on either side of our estimated date."

If nothing else, he was certainly thorough. "Maybe the record is simply closed—"

"Only from the other side, from the birth mother's side, would any information be kept confidential."

She knew that. Still, she'd love to put together a scenario that would allow Diane at least hope of a legal adoption. Jennifer sighed. "So where'd she come from?"

Sam helped himself to a slug of her water and raked back his hair. "Hey, I'm a newspaper reporter, not a seer. Maybe you should ask Valerie."

He was kidding, but if, for one moment, she thought Valerie could conjure up the truth about Diane, she would ask her to do just that.

"It's not like this child was an infant," Jennifer reminded him. "Someone would miss a three-year-old."

"So you're saying you think she was stolen?"

"Well, let's look at this as logically as possible," she suggested, fingering the sugar packets in the small glass container in the middle of the table. "How does a young child become available for adoption?"

"Her parents can no longer take care of her because of illness, drug abuse, lack of means to support her, or—"

"Death," Jennifer finished, shoving the container to one side. "Only if any of those situations occurred, she should have gone into the child social services system, and, according to you, she didn't."

"At least not that I could find. And, believe me, I did try. A name would have helped."

"Okay then, let's look at what we can conclude. If Diane was adopted, it was out of state. If she is actually from Georgia, as her parents have led her to believe both they and she are, the adoption must have been illegal."

"Most likely. We still have the question of how she wound up in Collier's hands."

He took another drink of water and then offered it back to her. As far as she was concerned, it was his now.

"Let's take this one step at a time," she suggested. "What about checking for a birth certificate?"

"I couldn't find one for a Diane Robbins in her age range, and there should be a corrected one if her name were changed."

"And the original?"

"Are you kidding? All we have is a first name of Cat. We aren't even sure how that should be spelled, with a C or a K, or what it might be short for. But I hardly think it's her given name. We certainly don't know her birth parents' names or, for sure, what her birth date is."

Jeez. He was such a stickler for details. "Okay, okay, so that's out."

"We're stabbing in the dark. If you really want to know the circumstances surrounding Diane's adoption, what we should do is find Diane's mother, the one that took off from Smith Mountain."

She could go with that.

"Get a license plate number, plus the make and model of her car, and I'll see what I can do. If she hasn't crossed state lines, we just might get lucky. "

"Will do."

"Good. You staying close to the apartment?"

His concern was nice, but she was a big girl, and what did she really have to be afraid of? "I'm doing what I have to do. The workmen are scheduled to install a new bedroom door in my apartment tomorrow. They had to order the lock I picked out for the front door. It'll take a few days for it to get here."

"One of those across-the-door steel jobbies like you see in movies about New York City, huh?"

"This is serious," she reminded him.

"I'm perfectly aware of that," he said, for once completely sober. "The police are pretty sure that Beverly Hoffman's death was a professional hit."

Jennifer tried to blink back her surprise as the waitress rounded the table and plopped down their orders, spilling some of the homemade potato chips onto the bare table. "Vanilla bean coffee was the closest I could get to regular today," she warned him, scooting a cup in Sam's direction and scooping up the wayward chips. He grunted and waved her away.

Jennifer stared at her sandwich with pepper and mushroom slices spilling out of the bun. Suddenly, she wasn't so hungry anymore.

"Professional?" she whispered.

Sam took a mammoth bite, tomato sauce clinging to one corner of his mouth. "The good news is that means they're most likely gone and won't be back. Made the hit, tried a recovery of the material—at the scene, at Diane's, and then at your place—all within a short period of time. Since we've had no more activity in more than twenty-four hours, I think we can assume these guys have left." He wiped the corner of his mouth with his napkin.

"Professional?" she repeated.

He waved the hand holding the napkin up and down in front of her face. She batted it away. "You weren't on the list. Neither was Johnny Zeeman. If he had been, they would have capped him in that alley."

"Capped him?"

"You know, put a bullet in his head. Made sure he was dead." He bit off another mouthful of meatballs. "They knew neither of you could make an ID. Too dark, and too far away."

She shoved her plate away. She might never eat again.

"Then why'd they come back up the alley looking for me?"

"You might have been armed, and they wanted to make sure Johnny was down. They weren't going to give you a chance to take them out." He grinned. "Of course, they didn't know it was *you* out there."

She made an ugly face at him.

"What you ought to be asking yourself is who hired them," he went on. "And how they knew to be in that alley that night. Who told them Hoffman was at the clinic to pass over information, assuming that's why she was killed."

Who, indeed? Johnny knew. So did Hoffman. And Diane. Who might they have told?

And where, exactly, was that information?

Chapter 15

The news that Beverly Hoffman's death could have been a hired kill left Jennifer on edge. Even though she was sure they were safe, she felt guilty for leaving the girls alone while she'd gone out for lunch with Sam.

A hand on her shoulder stopped Jennifer cold as she scurried across the parking lot toward Sam's apartment. She crouched, whirled, and let out a loud *hah-yah!* ready to do battle, but Johnny Z's "Hey, hey, watch it, will ya" kept her from landing what promised to be an anemic blow to his chest.

"One of these days I'm not going to be able to pull my punch," she barked at him.

He snickered at her. "Yeah, well save it for the enemy, doll."

Unfortunately, at this point, that might include him.

He leaned in and added, "We need to talk." He looked better than usual. His color was almost back to normal, at least what passed for his yellowish kind of normal, but his breath was cloying with smoke. At least he'd put on a suit and tie—a seedy suit and tie—but still . . .

"Haven't you ever heard of a telephone?" she asked, and then wondered why she'd bothered. He ignored every question she ever asked him.

"The girls all right?" He nodded in the direction of Sam's balcony.

"I left them well-supplied with pizza and videos. What more could a couple of teenage girls want?" Other than teenage boys.

"They can wait," he told her. "You and me have business to conduct. I thought maybe you might like some lunch. I know a nice, quiet, little place . . ."

Please, someone, tell her he wasn't asking her out. The suit. She should have known.

"Sorry. I've already eaten."

"Maybe some other time . . ."

And maybe not.

She leaned against the wrought-iron handrail that led up the steps, ready for some answers of her own. "I've got a question for you: Who'd you tell we'd be in that alley Sunday night?"

"Oh, I get it. You think I tipped somebody off, so I could get myself shot."

When he put it that way, it did sound pretty ridiculous.

"Any more questions?" he added, bristling that she'd had the nerve to ask. Or from her rejection. Maybe a little of both.

"Yeah, one. How'd you get yourself kicked off the Macon police force?"

His eyes narrowed, and for a moment he looked like he'd been sucker punched. "Tell you what," he said, "I'll answer that one if you want to explain how you got yourself charged with murder a few months back."

Her cheeks went red. He was playing dirty. But then, so was she. "It wasn't murder—"

"All right, then, communicating threats."

"You checked up on me." She felt violated, even if the story had been in all the newspapers.

"Like I said before, it's my job. You think I'd let just anyone in on my business? Besides, I've been asking myself who you might have told. Now, any more questions?"

She shook her head.

"Good. So what's Diane said about her parents?"

"Where they live, what they do."

"She tell you they can't be located?"

"Yeah. Her dad's on a business trip and her mom split."

"Panicked and cut out, huh?"

Jennifer shook her head at him. "Hardly."

"What you got in mind?" Johnny was reaching for another cigarette. If he kept this up, she'd have to check into buying some of those little filter masks to wear over her nose.

"Someone wants a child so badly they go through years of fertility treatments and then all the trouble of adopting her, maybe even illegally, and then they find out this kid is in some kind of trouble. My bet is she's already here in Macon looking for Diane."

His lighter wouldn't strike, so he chewed on the filter. "So what say we do a little nosing around Lanier, find out if someone's been asking after Diane."

As if she already didn't have more to do than there were hours in the day.

"And you don't think we might stand out a little too much, poking around on campus? It's not like anyone would mistake us for a couple of students."

"Not me, but you're somethin' else. Notch down that sophistication a level, and you could pass for twenty easy."

She didn't know if he was handing her a line to get what he wanted or whether he meant it, but it sure beat someone calling her ma'am.

"So you think she figures Diane will come back to the dorm or show up in class, and when she does . . ." Johnny waved his hand.

"She'll be there," Jennifer finished.

"I could go with that."

"Well, I'm not quite sure I'm ready to deal with Mrs. Robbins. Besides, I think we won't have to go looking for her. Most likely, one way or another, she'll find us," Jennifer told him. "Moms are like that."

"Yeah? Well, when she does, I'm counting on you to gain her trust."

"Me?"

"Sure. She's a lot more likely to listen to a nice-looking, friendly gal like you than she is someone like me."

At least they could agree on that.

"And when you do, see if you can't get her to give you one of her bank deposit slips."

"Oh, and just how am I supposed to do that?"

"Ask for her address. If it doesn't occur to her, suggest that it's printed on a deposit slip. Most people figure the only way you could use it is to put money in the bank."

"How else can you use it?" she asked.

"Just see if you can get it and hope that she turns up soon."

"Why?"

"She's got to know something."

Chapter 16

When Jennifer left Johnny and finally got up to Sam's apartment, the girls were getting restless. They weren't used to captivity. She studied them as they lounged on the floor. They were drinking Cherry Cokes.

Diane was quiet, remote, pouty. She'd forgone the dark red lipstick and most of the eyeliner. She looked younger than before, almost like she was drawing back into her childhood, back to when she was safe, sometime after three and before seventeen.

They'd let Muffy finish off the pizza crusts they'd thrown back into the box they left on the floor. Jennifer let her have the last piece, then crumpled the cardboard and stuck it in the trash can.

"Why didn't you bring any of our CDs?" Valerie moaned at Diane. "Did you take a look at the kind of music Sam listens to? Arrrrgghhh."

She flung herself out flat on the floor, her fiery orange-red hair spread out like a starburst, and stared back up over her eyebrows at Jennifer. "Surely you have something better at your place."

"Like what?"

"Like Cake."

"Cake? I thought you wanted music."

Valerie groaned louder this time and covered her eyes.

86

"What century are these people from? How long did you say we had to stay here?"

"I thought you liked it here," Diane snapped, apparently more irritated with Valerie than she was with being at Sam's apartment.

"It's not that; it's just I need to get out," Valerie insisted, sitting up and stretching her legs.

"Well, there's the door. No one's got you locked in," Diane hissed.

They *were* getting on each other's nerves. Bored, tired, and confined: a dangerous combination. TV and the Internet held only so much appeal.

"I don't think going out would be such a good idea, at least not yet," Jennifer suggested.

Diane nudged her toward the bedroom. Once they were inside, she shut the door and leaned against it. "She's been doing tarot spreads all morning. The girl thinks she's a wiccan."

"A witch?" Jennifer shook her head. "She's just playing." Or so she hoped. "Where'd she get the cards?"

Diane gave her a look. "She carries them in her purse, can you believe it? So, tell me she's not into this stuff. She actually looked through all of Sam's closets and drawers to see if he had a Ouija board. My dad always says you shouldn't mess with that stuff. Never know what you might call up."

"So did mine. Invites trouble," Jennifer agreed. "But Valerie seems harmless enough. How'd the two of you meet?"

She shrugged. "She came with the room." Diane crossed behind her and sat on the foot of Sam's unmade bed.

Men. He should have made it up. After all, he knew there was company in the house. Jennifer came around the side, tugged the comforter out from under Diane, and threw it over the sheets.

"What are we going to do? I can't stay here forever. I've got classes." She chewed on one dark red fingernail.

At least she was diligent. It hadn't been much more than a day, but it hardly seemed a good idea to point that out. In college terms, that could be over a hundred pages of reading.

"Johnny's doing what he can," Jennifer assured her. "So is Sam, and I've got a friend setting something up. We *will* figure it out."

"Good, but I've got a full scholarship that requires a 3.0 grade average to keep. I didn't even bring my books." She reached behind her for Sam's pillow and hugged it to her, like a child holding on to a teddy bear.

"Hey, I'm impressed. What were you, valedictorian of your high school class?" Jennifer asked, hoping to get her talking about something more pleasant.

Diane frowned at her. "Nothing like that, but I did all right. Got B's mostly. Private colleges have a lot more latitude than public universities. They give out a lot of special-type awards, especially for specific majors."

"And your major is . . ."

"I don't know yet."

Okay. This conversation seemed at a dead end, but at least they were talking. She needed Diane to trust her. "So how'd you wind up in Macon?"

She shrugged. "It was Mom's idea, mostly, I guess. We scoped out a few schools, mainly in state, but some in Tennessee and North Carolina. But this scholarship came along, and Mom said that was it. Lanier has a great reputation as a liberal arts school, and since I still don't know what I want to go into, she thought it was the best choice."

"When you talked to the nurse at the clinic, did you tell her who you were?" Jennifer asked casually.

She shook her head. "I didn't really talk to her. I was so freaked out, all I wanted was out of there."

"But did you mention you went to Lanier?"

"Valerie might have. What are you getting at?"

"Johnny had to give her your name, otherwise she wouldn't have known what was going on. It just struck me that she probably realized you were a college student, even if he didn't tell her."

But that didn't explain how someone knew she was at Lanier instead of Mercer or Wesleyan or Macon College.

Diane looked up from where she'd been twisting the corner of Sam's pillowcase. "What difference would that make?"

Maybe none, and maybe why her dorm room had been ransacked. She was learning from Johnny Z. She didn't answer.

"I don't suppose you have a picture of your mother with you?"

Diane blinked at her. "I think I still have one in my wallet, the one Mom and Dad had taken for their church directory." She dug in the back pocket of her jeans, pulled out her wallet, flipped through it, and handed Jennifer a bent, two-by-three-inch photo.

Her parents were an attractive, young-looking couple with big smiles. Her mother was blond, most likely an attempt to cover the gray. Her straight, one-length hair curled under at her shoulders. Her father, graying at the temples, seemed pleasant enough.

"You're not in the picture," she observed.

Diane's eyes narrowed. "I don't go to church that much." She definitely had Jennifer pegged as one of the "grown-ups."

"Mind if I borrow this?" she asked.

"I want it back," Diane told her.

"I promise."

"Why do you need it?"

"We think your mom might be in Macon," Jennifer explained.

Diane rolled her eyes. Again.

"You don't look surprised."

"Are you kidding? That woman's on me twenty-four, seven. If she's not home, you can bet she's here somewhere. Either that or she's gone to get my dad. She doesn't think I know how to breathe without her."

Diane dumped the pillow and started unraveling the fringe on the throw that lay at the foot of the bed.

"You and your mom don't get along?"

Diane shrugged. "It's just that's she's always in my business."

Jennifer nodded. She thought it better not to point out that a mother's business *was* her children.

"Look. I've got a paper due next week in my survey of English lit class. And if I get too far behind in math—"

"Okay, message sent and received. I'll get over to Lanier as soon as I can and pick up your books. Make me a list."

"I need the rest of my makeup and some clean clothes and—"

The telephone rang and Jennifer lifted the receiver. But before she could speak, another voice chimed in with "Hello."

"I've got it, Valerie," Jennifer said. There was a pause. "I've got it," she repeated, relieved to hear the clunk of the receiver falling into its cradle.

"I've been calling all over Macon for you." It was Teri. "Even tried Mrs. Walker in Atlanta. Your answering machine isn't picking up, and Dee Dee has no idea where you are. I don't suppose you'd like to tell me what you're doing at Sam's when he's at work? And who was that woman who answered the phone?"

"I told you. Someone broke into—"

"And because of that you're shackin' up with Sam?"

She turned her back on Diane in an effort to get at least a modicum of privacy and whispered into the phone. "I am *not* shackin'—"

"Whatever. But you know better. Guys like him don't come along every day. You two have too much going for you to blow it. You've got to ease into this one, girl. Moving in with him casually—"

"I haven't moved in. I'm a guest as in staying with, not living with. Got that? And there's nothing casual about it. Two armed men broke into my home, stormed my bedroom, threatened me with bodily harm—"

"Oh, my God. You didn't tell me all that. I thought you meant somebody lifted your TV. You mean they actually—"

"No, they didn't, but they would have if they had gotten through the bedroom door and if Mrs. Thorne didn't have a vendetta against loud music. I'm fine."

"Sometimes you don't make much sense. Is Muffy all right?"

"She's fine, too."

"Good. I still don't know why you didn't come to my place to stay."

As if Teri would be any kind of protection.

"So tell me," Teri said, "what *have* you and Sam been doing?"

Jennifer let out an exasperated puff of air. "Why did you call?"

"Oh, that. We have an appointment Thursday afternoon at 5:45 at the fertility clinic. You're to meet us there."

"Meet who?"

"Me and Monique. She's the one with the problem. Poor thing's been trying for twenty years to have a baby and just can't seem to make it happen. Figure out what you are to her before you get there, and make it believable. Maybe her daughter."

"You just told me she's infertile."

"Oh, that's right. Niece then, whatever. Make it good."

"But I told you, someone there might recognize me."

"Not likely. You won't be wearing slime. Besides, with Monique in the room, I hardly think anyone will be looking at you. She knows how to take center stage."

She had a point.

"Besides," Teri added, "Monique said she wouldn't do it unless you were there. We'll protect you."

Like that was some kind of reassurance.

"How'd you manage to get an appointment so soon?"

"Monique made it. They're working us in. Need I say more?"

Not really.

"Okay. I'll see you then," Jennifer agreed.

"No, wait. I almost forgot. You're to be at Monique's tonight, seven sharp."

"Any special reason?"

"She's called the whole gang in—you, me, Leigh Ann, even April. She's not happy about what happened."

"You didn't tell her about my apartment being broken into, did you?"

"Only a little. I didn't know the juicy part."

Jennifer groaned. "So she's calling a meeting?"

"That's what she said. Apparently 'the situation is more serious' than she first thought."

Where did Monique get off taking over her life? Probably the same place Teri did. "Well, I don't feel under any obligation to go."

The pause on the line was not good.

"You still want to get published one of these days?" Teri asked. Jennifer could almost see her impatiently tapping her foot. "I wouldn't alienate Monique if I were you. She means well, and, Jennifer, she really does know what she's doing."

Maybe about writing, but her own personal life was quite another matter.

"Don't upset her," Teri warned. "She's only trying to do right by you. I think she sort of thinks of all of us as family."

It was true, and she *had* asked for help. She just wasn't sure she could handle two nights in a row of Teri, Leigh Ann, Monique, and April. "All right. I'll be there."

"Good." Teri was back to her overenergized self. "See you tonight."

Chapter 17

It might not have been the Spanish Inquisition, but dim the lights a little and give Monique one of those robes, and it would have been hard to tell the difference.

"You have the skills, Jennifer," Monique insisted. "Use them."

Put an echo to those words, and she could have sworn Obi-Wan Kenobi had spoken. She should be so lucky.

If all Monique intended to accomplish with this meeting was to alternately browbeat and inspire her into devising a plot for the real-life mystery she was drowning in, she could have done it by e-mail. But then, Monique probably wanted to make sure she didn't have access to that wonderful invention, the delete button.

Besides, if Monique wrote mystery, she'd understand that those carefully inspired flashes of insight her sleuths came up with were the result of careful manipulation of her characters. How could any kind of fictional scenario have any relevance to what was going on in her real life?

Jennifer had told them everything she knew about Diane, her mother, the adoption, and Beverly Hoffman's death, which wasn't much. Going over it again wasn't going to change her story. She still didn't know what was going on.

"Babies," April said, patting her tummy as if using it

as a visual aid. "It seems to me, this whole thing is about babies." She shifted uncomfortably on the couch.

Of course, at the moment everything seemed to be about babies to April. And no wonder, that kid seemed far too fond of his or her current situation and in no hurry to make his debut, regardless of any discomfort he might be affording his mother.

"I can see why you'd think that," Leigh Ann offered from the safety of the corner section of Monique's sofa. She had been surprisingly quiet while Monique bullied, Teri sympathized, and April made her increasing discomfort known. "But I think what's going on with Diane is all about identity."

"Oh, come on," Teri chimed in, rolling her eyes. "For all practical purposes this Diane person knows who she is—Diane Robbins. Okay, so she was raised with a name other than her birth name. So what? It's not like she lost her memory and forgot her life. She lived it. 'What's in a name?' Besides, how many memories do any of us have before the age of three anyway?"

"Do you really want to know?" Leigh Ann asked. "I was regressed once, all the way back to the womb. I remember my first Christmas, my first birthday, my first boyfriend—"

"Before age three? Girl, you *are* sick," Teri declared. She turned to Jennifer. "So, you thinkin' about having Diane regressed?"

Jennifer shook her head. "She's too fragile for that. Besides, those kind of recovered memories are suspect." She threw a pointed look in Leigh Ann's direction. "What we need are facts. We've already got too many maybes.

"But Leigh Ann has a point," Jennifer added. "Diane's situation *is* about identity. We want to know who she is, who her biological parents are."

"Yeah, but I think you're looking at this all backward," Leigh Ann explained. "You keep asking who she is when you should be asking why is it *important* who she is."

"Are you following any of this?" Teri asked April.

"Not a word. Think you could slip a pillow under my leg if I can get it up?"

Teri stole the one from behind Leigh Ann and, with Monique's help, wedged it under April's knee.

"Look," Leigh Ann said, sitting forward. "If any of us found out we'd been adopted, so what? I mean, except on an emotional level, who would care? There might be lots of tears, feelings of betrayal and loss, but no one would be running around shooting people in alleys or passing secret information back and forth. You think it's because she was *adopted*. I'm saying what if it's because *she* was adopted. Different stress from the verb to the noun. Get my drift?"

"Yeah, and it's a valid point. But we're dealing with murder here," Jennifer insisted, "which means the most likely answer is an illegal operation, people making money by selling babies. Big bucks being passed back and forth."

"Are we? Where's your proof? Where are the other babies?" Leigh Ann asked, a little too satisfied with herself.

"That's what we intend to find out during our little excursion Thursday," Jennifer pointed out, "the one in which we uncover proof the East Lake Fertility Clinic is a cover for a black market baby operation."

"If you're going to start talking about selling babies, I'm going home," April declared.

"Even if we were to get some kind of hint that the clinic was indeed delving into a kind of black market," Monique stated, leaning forward in her rocking chair, "I don't see how that would provide proof. I hardly think

Dr. Collier is going to break down and hand us a written contract."

"I'm not talking about proof we can take to the authorities, at least not yet," Jennifer insisted.

"Yeah. We get Collier to say something in front of witnesses—that would be the three of us," Teri said pointing to herself, Jennifer, and Monique, "and we'll get the FBI to send us back in wired."

Terrific. Now Teri had them in the middle of an undercover government sting.

"Stands to reason," she went on, "the feds have been watching them for some time, waiting for someone like us to break the whole mess wide open."

"I don't think so," Jennifer said. "As a matter of fact, I'm not sure but what we shouldn't call the whole thing—"

"Thursday, 5:45," Monique repeated. "You two meet me in the parking lot ten minutes early. Now go home."

They were dismissed, just like that. Like it or not, Jennifer would have to go through with it. If she didn't, she'd never hear the end of it.

Chapter 18

Jennifer's heart caught in her throat as she drove her little Volkswagen Beetle into the parking lot of Sam's apartment. A police car was parked in the dim light of the street lamp next to the steps. No lights were flashing, but the sight was every bit as terrifying as if sirens had been blaring and the sidewalks roped off. Quickly, she pulled into one of the two remaining spaces next to the road.

Every conceivable horror tumbled through her brain. If something had happened to Diane, she'd never forgive herself. She'd left the girls alone to go to Monique's, before Sam had gotten home. Why had she been so foolish, so overconfident that they were safe? Johnny had warned her, warned her that if he'd found her, then someone else—

She couldn't let herself think about all that. *Stay focused,* she told herself as she jerked on the emergency brake and pulled the keys from the ignition with sweaty, uncooperative fingers. No use speculating, when in just a few moments she'd know. She practically stumbled to the steps.

The girls were sulking in the living room. Neither speaking to the other, but lots of body language was going on. Sitting on the floor near the coffee table trunk with her knees drawn to her chest, Diane looked up through that strangely red hair as Jennifer came in. Valerie, standing near the table on the other side of the room, stuck her hands in the rear pockets of her jeans, turned her back, and struck a pose, as if to say, "Don't mess with me."

Over near the kitchen, Sam was huddled with Tim Donahue, in full police uniform. They were friends from way back. She'd always suspected he was one of Sam's major sources, but neither one would admit it.

Sam caught her eye and raised a wait-one-minute finger.

At least everyone was accounted for, including Muffy, who saw fit to bathe Jennifer's hands in doggy saliva, apparently glad, at last, for a friendly face. Everyone else was too preoccupied to give her the attention she obviously deserved.

Some of the tension drained from Jennifer's body. Whatever was going on, at least no one had been hurt. Her mom had taught her to count her blessings: all present, one; no blood, two.

"She walked out," Diane told Jennifer without even a hello.

Jennifer tossed her bag in a corner and squatted down next to Diane. "What do you mean?"

"I was sleeping, and she took off. No note, no nothin'. Didn't even lock the door." She shot a dagger in the other girl's direction.

Valerie whirled. "I went out for a damn doughnut. So sue me." She punched the Dunkin' Donuts bag on the table.

"Why didn't you lock the door?" Jennifer asked.

"I didn't have a damn key, and I didn't want to wake Diane up coming back in. I wasn't gone more than fifteen minutes. Christ, you'd think I'd massacred a village."

"Just cool it," Jennifer cautioned.

"Cool it? *Excuse* me. He called the cops." Valerie pointed at Sam.

The two men turned and Tim spoke. "Miss, in the future, leave a note when you go out. You could save everybody a lot of worry." He let himself out the door, turning back for one last smile and to add, "You ladies have a nice evening." He patted Muffy, who felt it her obligation to see everybody out as well as in. Part of her hostessing duties.

"He called the police because he was worried about you," Jennifer said, watching Sam's pensive face.

Some of Valerie's anger fell away. "I know. Look, I'm really sorry. This place was getting on my nerves, and I just needed to get some air. If Sam had gotten home twenty minutes later, you'd never have known I was gone."

"You want me to take you back to your dorm?" Sam offered. "Whatever's going on doesn't concern you. The dean could find you another room."

She shook her head, her face blanching. "Nah. I don't want to leave Diane by herself. But maybe you could give me a key . . ."

"No key. If you stay, you don't go out unless Jen or I know it. Understood?"

She nodded. "Understood." She went over to Diane and put a hand on her arm. "Hey, roomie, I bought you a doughnut. Your favorite, Boston cream."

Diane stared up at her. "You don't get off that easy."

"Okay. What do you say I make it two creams and throw in a blueberry?"

"And a handful of chocolate doughnut holes?"

"Boy, you don't ask for much."

"Deal?"

"Deal."

And with that, they made up. Jennifer only wished she could shake the hollow feeling in her stomach as easily.

Someone would miss a three-year-old. Jennifer stared at her computer screen resting on the dining table, the brightness glowing eerily in the dark. The girls were asleep on the floor, Sam in his room. Even Muffy had given up and was whimpering in her sleep. Chasing rabbits, her dad had always said.

A three-year-old. Jaimie wasn't more than a dream, yet Jennifer knew that if she or he were ever born and if he or she were to vanish, she would never rest until she'd found her child. Never.

Most of the missing children listed at the Web site had been abducted by family members or had disappeared as teenagers. Probably runaways, but who knew? Their parents could only hope that one day they'd call or turn up. But the little ones, the ones who couldn't possibly take care of themselves, what hope was there for them?

She plugged in the little information she knew about Diane. Female. White. Brown eyes. Her hair was most likely brown, but who knew under that dye, and besides, it could have been lighter as a child. She left the hair as *any*. Age now: zero to twenty. She typed in *Cat* under first name and hit Search. NO MATCHES.

She deleted *Cat* and got 123 matches. Back to the main menu, she inserted *nonfamily abduction* and hit Enter. A page of sixteen names and photos appeared. Most had gone missing as older children, but there were three possibilities: Lori Jean Miller, Cynthia Allison Turner, and Tiffany Elizabeth Stevens, all missing at age three. She'd expected to find a lot more, but surely not every case was posted on the net. None shared Diane's birth date, November 1.

She highlighted Lori Jean Miller and hit Enter. Her

"poster" came up. Born July 18. Last seen playing in her front yard. Philadelphia, PA.

Cynthia Allison Turner. Born August 14. Not found at crime scene of parents' murder/suicide. Bethesda, MD.

Tiffany Elizabeth Stevens. Born June 22. Mother and child missing from supermarket parking lot. Blood found in car. Wilmington, NC.

She stared at the age-enhanced photos, but Diane could have been any of them or none of them. All she was doing was making herself ill. It was too easy to take on other people's tragedies. Every one of these children needed to be found, to be reunited with their families or, at least, to come to some kind of closure. She couldn't help them, and it looked like she couldn't help Diane.

She bookmarked the site and turned off the computer, frustrated, tired, and fed up. She had to get some sleep. She'd had precious little these last days, and she had Beverly Hoffman's funeral to get through tomorrow.

She rearranged the blankets of her bedroll and lay down, Diane and Valerie, their breathing even, not much more than an arm's length away.

The floor was hard, but she hardly noticed. Her mind was elsewhere, lost somewhere in the grief of separation, child from parent, the one truly unconditional love. She turned on her pillow, and the tears flowed silently down her cheeks.

Muffy stirred, stretched, and sauntered over. She lay down next to her, nuzzling her in the darkness. Jennifer burrowed her face in the dog's short fur and wept.

Chapter 19

Beverly Hoffman had conveniently died on a Sunday, making Wednesday afternoon, when the clinic was closed to make up for late Friday night hours, the perfect time for her funeral. Her service was held at the First Presbyterian Church. Good thing, too. It was big enough to house the regular congregation plus a whole lot of curiosity seekers.

Jennifer arrived a full hour before the two o'clock service, so she could scope out the church prior to taking up post at the far back corner of the sanctuary. It gave her an unobstructed view as the mourners filed in.

According to Hoffman's obituary in the morning's newspaper, she was survived by her husband, Wayne, two children, and her parents, Mr. and Mrs. Aaron Billings. She'd received her B.S. degree in nursing and immediately gone to work for the East Lake Fertility Clinic. She was active in both church and PTA. No siblings were listed.

Someone, most likely the husband, had gone to a lot of expense. The casket, draped in a blanket of roses, was polished walnut with brass fittings. It was closed, of course. Dozens of floral arrangements crowded about it.

As the mourners began to arrive, Jennifer pulled down the wide brim of her black hat. In her black crepe dress and gloves, it was unlikely anyone would recognize her, and that was just the way she wanted it. She was there to observe. Murderers always attended their victims' funerals, especially in a murder-for-hire case when they thought they had nothing to fear. It was a cardinal rule of the mystery genre, so all she had to do was take careful note of who was there that day, and she'd have her list of suspects. She'd even brought along a pencil and pad tucked into the pocket of her skirt.

It didn't take long for the church to fill. Most of the press were there, although she had no idea where Sam was. He told her he was coming.

She did spy Lieutenant Schaeffer and one or two other policemen she recognized. All were out of uniform, properly attired, properly subdued, and, no doubt, toting their own notebooks.

Five minutes before two the family was ushered down the aisle to the front of the church. Paul Collier, supporting a middle-aged man who looked confused and disoriented, led the way. They were followed by a woman in a navy-blue suit and white blouse who, arms linked, walked between an older couple. They had to be Beverly's parents. Directly behind, carrying a small girl and holding the hand of a young boy, was a man who was an echo of Paul, taller, less stocky, with darker hair than Paul's graying mane. He had to be Donald, the younger brother. A lanky young man who could have been twenty or so was close behind.

Another couple followed, but she had no idea who they might be.

Jennifer felt warm air tickle her neck and jerked back, bumping into someone. She spun around. Sam stood behind her grinning like he'd caught her stealing candy.

He wore a charcoal suit and looked really sharp. She hadn't seen him when he left the apartment that morning. She'd been trying to make up for some of those late night hours by sleeping in.

"At least you didn't bring a stepladder," he said. "Maybe you could try climbing up on one of the pews if you need a better look."

She scowled. "How'd you know where to find me?"

"I simply asked myself what Jennifer would wear to a funeral. And then I saw this gorgeous woman hiding behind a big black hat and standing alone in the back of the church. Not too many hats and not so much black these days, mostly navy-blue and brown. Besides, I knew you'd be here. The gloves are a nice touch, by the way."

He leaned in as though imparting some great words of wisdom. "Murderers don't really attend the funerals of their victims."

Her cheeks reddened. He thought he was so smart.

"I'm paying my respects," she said. "I was the one who found her. It only seems right." That much was true. Even if she hadn't wanted a look at the attendees, Jennifer would have felt an obligation to see Beverly Hoffman to her final rest. As long as she lived, she'd never get the sight of those strange, dead eyes out of her mind. Just thinking about it made her shudder.

"You all right?" Sam asked.

She nodded, shaking off the image. "Do you have any idea who's with the family up there?" She pointed toward the second pew.

"That's Paul Collier with Beverly's husband Wayne. And Mrs. Collier sitting between Beverly's parents, the Billingses. The children with Donald Collier belong to Beverly and Wayne. The young man is one of Paul's sons. He's a senior at Mercer this year. The thin man with the cavernous cheeks is McEvoy. The short white-haired woman clinging to his arm is his wife. And the tall woman with the gray bun at her neck who's joining them right now is Dr. Sullivan."

"Really? So Sullivan is a woman."

"Certainly seems that way."

"You get any more on Hoffman?"

"Yeah. Convinced my editor to let me do a profile of her for the paper. Makes good copy sometimes and gives me an official reason to go poking around. From all accounts, she was as nice a person as you'd want to meet. She'd been working at the clinic for about sixteen years or so. Everybody liked her—colleagues and patients alike."

"I know they worked together, but why are the Colliers sitting with the family?"

"I thought you knew. They *are* family. Beverly was Mrs. Collier's niece." He pointed at the pew. "That couple she's sitting between are her sister and her brother-in-law."

"But they look older—"

"They are. Mrs. Collier is the youngest of a brood of eight."

The organ music stopped and the minister stepped up behind the lectern.

Sam touched her arm and whispered, "I'll talk to you later." Then he disappeared before she could reply.

It was just as well. She didn't want anyone seeing them together. Too many people knew they were friends, and she hadn't gone to all the trouble of making sure no one would recognize her to have him give her away now. Besides, she could digest only so many family connections at one time.

Her own family had been about as simple as they come. Just her and her parents and a distant cousin here and there.

Jennifer continued to scan the crowd as the pastor

welcomed the group, the soothing tones of his tenor suddenly breaking her concentration.

"We are here to say goodbye to our sister Beverly whose time on this earth was far too short . . ."

The words rang so familiar. Suddenly she was bathed in an unexpected, debilitating wave of sadness. She felt as if she were suffocating, as if every ounce of strength had been sucked from her body.

This was the first funeral she'd attended since she'd laid her parents to rest, more than seven years ago. She had thought she would be all right, but the wound was still too fresh, would probably always be too fresh. She missed them so much her chest ached. What did she think she was doing, chasing after murderers? She felt far too young, too vulnerable, too alone.

She needed her parents to tell her that everything was going to be all right. To tell her what she was doing right, what she was doing wrong. She needed them to love her back, love her absolutely and unconditionally as they had all their lives, right up until the moment when they were gone. So finally, so irrevocably gone.

Tears washed her eyes as she awkwardly pulled herself to her feet, stumbled out of the pew, and ran on tiptoe toward the high, arched doors open at the rear of the church, toward sunlight and fresh air.

And directly into a tall blond woman with shoulder-length hair.

Jennifer apologized, pulling off her hat and gloves and dabbing at her eyes with a well-worn tissue she found in her purse. She leaned back against the stone front of the church, the sun shining on her face, while she took in great breaths of air.

"She must have been a relative of yours," the woman said, stepping out of the doorway. Her face was drawn and lined.

"No, I . . ." Jennifer swallowed hard and, feeling enormously foolish, almost laughed. "I'm afraid funerals and I don't get along."

For the first time, she took a good look at the woman. She looked remarkably familiar. Remarkably, in fact, like the photo she had in her purse.

"You're Diane's mother," she said before she'd had a chance to consider whether it might be a bad idea to let this woman know she recognized her.

The woman's eyes brightened.

"Thank God, yes," she said. "You know her. Do you know where she is?"

Jennifer nodded, suddenly more sure than anything else that Anne Marie Robbins was the one person who would help Diane.

Chapter 20

Anne Marie Robbins was a wreck. Jennifer wondered how she'd managed to drive all the way from Smith Mountain to Macon without causing some major damage to herself or someone else.

"She's fine, really," Jennifer assured her, pushing a coffee cup in her direction and then the creamer and the sugar. Maybe if she would only drink something, it would calm her nerves. Jennifer suspected the woman hadn't eaten a full meal in days, but Anne Marie refused to order more than a drink. They were sitting in a booth at the Nu-Way Restaurant, a couple of blocks from the church.

Jennifer glanced at her watch. The service was still going on. The procession to Rose Hill Cemetery wouldn't start for at least another twenty minutes.

"I've left so many messages on her answering machine, the tape has run out," Mrs. Robbins was saying.

Her eyelids were ringed with red, and Jennifer could see where she'd put a little too much concealer under her eyes.

"I didn't know where else to go. She hasn't been back to her dorm room in days. And then I saw the obituary in today's paper. I've been checking them each day, just in case. . . ."

"You recognized the name of the clinic."

Mrs. Robbins nodded.

"There was an incident at the dorm—" Jennifer began.

"Oh, my God." What little color there was in the woman's face completely disappeared.

"No. I've told you she's fine. Someone searched her room. That's all." The woman's eyes again grew huge, and Jennifer quickly added, "While she was gone. She's been staying with me."

Mrs. Robbins looked totally confused. Jennifer dug in her purse and produced the photo as if it somehow validated her connection with Diane.

The woman studied it and then looked up. "But why you?"

Excellent question, and one not easily answered in twenty words or less. "She hired a private detective. I've been helping him out."

"Diane told me about the detective, this Johnny Zeeman character. I went by his office this morning, but he wasn't there. Bad part of town. She should never have gotten herself mixed up with someone like that. She's only a child."

"She needs to know who she is," Jennifer insisted, briskly stirring her own coffee.

Anne Marie looked straight at her. "I'll tell you who she is. She's my daughter. She needs *my* help, not some stranger's. I want you to take me to her. Now."

Jennifer shook her head. Diane could have taken off for Smith Mountain the minute she realized that something was wrong, but she didn't. She'd headed for Johnny Z's, a point she thought better not shared with Mrs. Robbins, but one that said a lot about how much Diane trusted her mother's ability to help her right now.

"Tell me first," Jennifer insisted. "Tell me how you came to adopt her. I know about the connection with the fertility clinic. I know she was three when you got her, I know her name was Cat, and," she held her breath for a second, "I know it was illegal."

She was bluffing, about knowing for sure the adoption was illegal and about keeping her from her daughter. As soon as she possibly could, she had every intention of re-uniting her with Diane because she was sure, for no good reason except the feeling in her heart, that this woman loved her daughter and would never do anything inten-tionally to harm her.

Anne Marie looked like she'd been punched in the stomach. "Does she know?" she managed to whisper.

"Only what you've told her," Jennifer assured her.

"I want to be the one."

Jennifer nodded. "I promise."

"Stew and I had consulted the clinic. We'd been trying to have a child for over six years, closer to seven actually. I was almost thirty-five. They couldn't help us, not and have it be our own child, genetically, I mean. And we'd run out of money. We couldn't take out any more loans. I was heartbroken." She put a hand over her mouth until she regained her composure. "Babies were almost non-existent for adoption, and the legalities of adopting an older child seemed endlessly complicated. We could have been foster parents, but I didn't think I could handle falling in love with a child and living with the fear she might someday be taken out of our home."

Jennifer dug in her purse, found a clean tissue this time, and passed it to Anne Marie.

"Paul called me late one night. He said he had a beau-tiful three-year-old girl who needed a home, but there was a catch. We could ask no questions, we were never to tell her she was adopted, and we would have to relo-cate from Macon immediately."

"But why relocate?"

"So we could establish a residence as though she were our natural child. A family moves into a neighborhood, no one asks if the children are their own."

"And you agreed? Just like that?"

"No, of course not. But he brought the child to our home. She was tiny, and so scared it made my heart ache. When I picked her up, she clung to me and wouldn't talk. He tried to pull her from me, but she dug her little fingers into my sweater. I knew I could never give her back. She was so afraid. He didn't say so, but I felt certain she was in danger."

"Did he give you any papers?"

"Yes, a birth certificate already filled out, listing our names as her parents. He had some papers for us to sign. I asked if it was legal, and he assured me it was. But I guess I always suspected they were forged. I just didn't let myself think about it. I was afraid of what might happen to her if we didn't take her."

"And your husband went along with this?"

"I didn't give him a choice. His business is such it doesn't really matter where we live. I suspect that's one of the reasons Paul called us."

"What about her biological parents?"

"I don't know. He didn't say."

"And you didn't ask?"

"I didn't dare."

"Didn't you care? She was three years old."

"Not enough. At least not then."

"How did you know her name was Cat?"

"When I called her Diane, the name on the birth certificate, she corrected me, told me her name was Cat. So we called her our little Diane Cat for a while and finally just Diane."

"Do you know of anyone else who . . ." How could she phrase this so she didn't alienate the woman? ". . . anyone else Paul Collier might have helped with adoption?"

"We asked no questions, just as Paul had said. I had what I wanted. I wasn't going to do anything to jeopardize my child. If I had thought for one moment that letting her come to Macon would bring all this back up . . ." Her voice choked up, and she waved the tissue at Jennifer.

"Okay. I want you to write down where you're staying. You might want to give me your home address as well while you're at it."

The woman searched through her purse for something to write on. "Have you got something . . ."

"How about one of your bank deposit slips," Jennifer suggested casually. "That would already have your address. You can simply add your motel and room number."

The woman stopped for a moment, as though considering if that would be all right, and then pulled out her checkbook, removed a slip from the back and scribbled something on it. Then she handed it to Jennifer.

"Great. I'll be in touch," Jennifer assured her, stuffing the paper into her bag.

The woman grabbed Jennifer's wrist. "You said you'd—"

"Make sure you see her. I will. I promise. But, Mrs. Robbins, one person has already died, and another was shot," she said gently. "I have to be sure that when you see her, Diane will be protected."

She'd have to come up with a meeting place that was both public enough to be safe and isolated enough to allow privacy.

"And why should I trust you?"

"Because you don't have a choice."

The woman nodded. She'd see her daughter soon, Jennifer vowed. She would see to it.

Chapter 21

"Well, this is a first." Dee Dee raised one eyebrow at Jennifer, who was dropping dumplings into a large pot of broth. "Since when did you come to, let alone volunteer at a Wednesday night church supper? I thought that when you went to a church, it was First Baptist."

"Your mom needs the help. She told me so over the phone. You couldn't expect her to set up tables for over two hundred people all by herself."

"She has help," Dee Dee told her with a sweeping glance around the huge kitchen buzzing with women chopping salad, pulling apple pies from one cavernous oven, checking on vegetable dishes, and extracting huge bowls of coleslaw, fruit salad, and various other food jumbles from the refrigerated units.

"I believe how she put it to me was, 'Jennifer wants to come to the Wednesday night church supper. What's she up to this time?'"

Jennifer stuck her chin out and continued dropping the soft dough into the broth. It foamed and rolled in the hot liquid.

"Where's the pepper?" she asked. "This stock's not going to be fit to eat if we don't find something around here to flavor it."

"Don't change the subject," Dee Dee warned. "Are you here because I told you Mrs. Collier was coming?"

Jennifer threatened Dee Dee with a large wooden spoon. "I'm here because . . . because . . ." It wasn't right to lie, especially not in church, even if it was only the kitchen. She always felt like God took it personally.

She could tell Dee Dee she was there because she'd hoped to take a decent home-cooked meal back to the girls, but Dee Dee didn't even know they were staying with her at Sam's.

"While you're trying to come up with a fib that you think you could technically classify as truth, you might want to cover that pot if you want those dumplings to cook right."

As Jennifer capped the pot with an ill-fitting metal lid, she said, "So, does brother Donald make these get-togethers?"

"Collier?"

Jennifer nodded, leaning back against the counter and watching Dee Dee mop up the broth she'd slopped on the stove top.

"Not since his wife died a couple of years back. Real sad story. She was very active in the Right to Life Movement although she never had any children of her own. And then to top off the irony, she died of ovarian cancer."

Jennifer winced. "Her husband was in the fertility business."

"Yeah. But she believed people shouldn't tamper with God's plans for them, not through abortion and not through fertility clinics." Dee Dee patted her shoulder. "Check out the door. Ruthie Collier has arrived."

She was wearing the same navy suit she'd had on at the funeral, complete with white silk blouse and pearl earrings. Her hair was brushed off her full face and her red cheeks and wrapped into a twist at the back. She had Dee Dee's mother, Fran, in a death grip of a hug.

The woman drew back but continued to hold both of Fran's hands. "Oh, darlin', you don't know what a relief it is to come here tonight!" Her voice boomed across the kitchen, so that anyone who was the least bit interested couldn't have failed to hear it. "What with all the goin's-on we've had down at that clinic—police every which way, in and out, in and out. It's been the most awful mess. Paul is just beside himself. He can hardly get any work done, and the clients . . . Well, I've been on the phone all day Monday, Tuesday, and even this mornin' trying to reassure them when I wasn't busy with the arrangements for the funeral for poor Bev. Wayne's too shaken to make a single decision. Can you believe it? Shot dead, a bullet straight through her throat. Lord o' mercy, it just makes your blood crawl to think of it."

Jennifer nudged Dee Dee. "You didn't tell me Mrs. Collier was such a great friend of your mom."

"She isn't. That's just Ruthie's way. She treats everybody like long lost kin."

Good. Maybe Jennifer could get herself adopted into the clan.

She wiped the flour on her hands onto her smudged, full-length apron and came up behind Fran. "How long should I leave those dumplings in to cook?"

Fran broke away from Ruthie and raised an eyebrow. It was obvious where Dee Dee got her attitude. "Use a toothpick to see if they're done, but turn off the fire before they're cooked all the way through. They'll have to sit awhile before we get this crowd fed."

Jennifer reached past her and offered Ruthie her hand. "Hi, I'm Jen," she said as bright-eyed and bubbly as a ten-year-old hoping to earn a scout badge.

Ruthie looked at her, puzzled. "I don't believe I've seen you before." She said it as if anyone who came to

First Presbyterian was supposed to make application through her.

"Just helping out tonight."

Fran gave Jennifer an enigmatic once-over and backed away. "I'd better check on those dumplings." She touched Ruthie's hand. "You hang in there. As they say, this, too, shall pass."

Ruthie rewarded her with a big smile and started to turn back toward the door.

Jennifer stopped her with, "Mrs. Collier."

The woman turned back, and Jennifer realized she'd better have one heck of a good reason for detaining her.

"Yes?"

"I've heard a lot about your husband's work," Jennifer began.

The woman smiled as if to say, So what?

"I have a friend who already has a child, two actually, but she'd like to have more. A lot of places would tell her to be thankful she has any, but that doesn't keep her from wanting another one."

That wasn't a lie. April loved her children more than life itself, and she did want more even if this latest one was giving her fits refusing to be born. Of course, fertility had never been an issue for April.

"Well, darlin', you just send her right over to the East Lake Fertility Clinic. We don't judge a person's motives or pretend to know what's best for them. You see those two young'uns out there?"

She pointed through the door to a little towheaded girl who looked to be about six and a boy closer to twelve, with spiked hair, who looked totally uncomfortable in a white dress shirt and black trousers.

"They're my two youngest. If it hadn't been for the clinic, I wouldn't have had a one. Now my oldest is scheduled to bless us with a grandbaby in three months.

And I have another one around here somewhere who's still in college, barely twenty years old, and already engaged. Some would say he's too young, but I say thank God for the miracles He grants us. Of course, sometimes He has to use real-life people to produce them."

"Is that what the clinic does, create miracles?"

Mrs. Collier pursed her lips for a moment, and Jennifer thought she detected a hint of sadness. Then the woman smiled, showing lots of perfectly capped teeth. "I suppose so. For some of us, our children are our lives. They have to be. Not everyone understands that, not even people who make those miracles happen."

She patted Jennifer's hand. "You send that friend of yours on over. Paul will tell her what can be done. He tells it like it is."

"You must really admire your husband," Jennifer said.

The smile slid from the woman's face. "Paul has given me almost everything I've ever wanted. You tell your friend, maybe he can give her what she wants, too."

And with that she left, leaving Jennifer with the impression that Ruthie Collier felt more like a client than a wife. She watched as Ruthie immediately latched on to a tall young man with a handsome profile. She turned back toward Jennifer, pointed, and mouthed, "He's mine," and then smiled broadly.

She knew what Paul had given Ruthie: her six children. But what was it that she'd wanted so much that Paul hadn't given her?

"I didn't find any chicken in this pot when I stirred it, Jennifer," Dee Dee said, brushing past her with oven mitts covering both hands and carrying the pot of dumplings. "Is this vegetable broth?"

"They'll never know the difference."

"I knew Mom shouldn't trust you."

"She said make dumplings. I made dumplings. It's not like you didn't fry enough chicken to keep the congregation in protein into the next millennium."

Dee Dee threw her a disgusted look. "So, you gonna stand there all day, or are you going to help?"

"Sure. What do you want me to do?"

"Grab whatever seems done in there and bring it out to the serving tables. And hurry. They're already queuing up."

Indeed, the line snaked down the side of the room and back between two rows of tables. She and Dee Dee were used to feeding a whole lot more people than this at one time, but with the number of cooks in the kitchen, the place was abuzz with confusion.

"Jennifer." Fran brought her up short. "Stand back out of the doorway. The ladies know exactly what to do."

She stepped back, and several women swept past with dishes. Fran handed her a dozen utensils. "You be responsible for taking in extra serving spoons. Any dish that doesn't have one, you stick it in. Since you made it, I'm going to put you to ladling out the chicken and dumplings. I've got Dee Dee on the lasagna. Lydia's handling the fried chicken, and Esther's covering the meatballs. Everyone can help themselves to the salads and vegetables. We have more than enough of those."

Sounded simple enough, but throw in lots of hungry kids, and it wasn't exactly the kind of catered party Jennifer was used to. But what the heck, if it took food to bring people together, then so be it. Fellowship was what it was all about, and if she had to pay for meeting Ruthie Collier by spooning up dumplings, she supposed it was a fair trade. Even if she hadn't learned a thing.

* * *

Dee Dee was two women over, behind the serving tables. She leaned out past Angie Watson and admonished Jennifer. "Don't serve a full scoop, and remember to put it in one of the upper corners, not the main compartment, otherwise they won't have room for much else. And if you get too much broth, it'll spill over into their vegetables and ruin everything."

As if she had never served before in her life. She'd been doing it for several years—with Dee Dee—and still Dee Dee never failed to think she had to tell her how. Fine. If she felt it necessary to exercise her Type A personality, that was okay. Jennifer just wished she were farther down the line, on the other side of Dee Dee. She felt sure that, at the end of the evening, she'd be getting a critique of her method.

Grace was said, and Fran opened the line. Jennifer made sure the dishes in front of her stayed neat and helped the little ones remember the green stuff.

In no time she found herself dipping from the bottom third of the pot. She glanced around to make sure she'd saved enough, and noticed Ruthie Collier, with four youngsters and the young college student she had claimed, coming up next. Two of the little ones asked for dumplings. They had little else on their plates.

"This is a family favorite," Ruthie assured her, offering her own for a serving. She looked at the plate as Jennifer handed it back to her. "Looks like you don't have much of the chicken left, but that's all right. The dumplings are the best part."

"That's right," Jennifer agreed.

The young man behind her, the one with the handsome profile, shoved his tray in her direction. Jennifer tilted the pot to get a decent scoop, looked up, and dropped her ladle into what was left of the mashed potatoes.

The young man, at first startled, drew back, recovering nicely. "Hey, that's okay," he assured her, obviously responding to the look of terror on her face. "I'll have something else."

All she could do was stammer, "I'm sorry, really, so sorry." But she couldn't tear herself from his face as he stared back at her.

With one blue eye and one brown.

Chapter 22

Isolated *and* public, those were the conditions Jennifer had put on a meeting place for Diane and Anne Marie Robbins. She could think of only one place in Macon that fit that description, the Ocmulgee National Monument on the east side of Macon, especially at eleven o'clock on a Thursday morning. Hardly anybody was around, except the park police, who kept a discreet presence, just in case.

It was one of Jennifer's favorite places to visit. Lots of luscious, well-cared-for rolling grass interrupted occasionally by man-made pyramidlike hills left by earlier inhabitants of the area. A peaceful place where the present tried hard not to intrude on a silent, mystical past.

Some of the mounds held secret chambers, only one of which was open to the public. Jennifer and Sam stood guard at the low, narrow, tunnel-like entrance that led to the meeting chamber where tribal leaders had met long ago to plan, to pray, to resolve their differences. It seemed like an apt place for mother and daughter to come to terms.

It was certainly better than a carousel at the local park at midnight. She'd seen that one done in so many movies she knew better than to step onto anything that moved when bad guys were after her. Running was one thing. Running in circles was quite another.

And she had the reassurance of bright sunshine. Everything—even death—looked less ominous in the daylight.

Sam paced the sidewalk, restless, obviously not at all sure Jennifer had made the right decision by bringing mother and daughter together so soon. He didn't really need to be there, but he'd insisted on coming, apparently so she could watch him fret. But then, he had that basic newspaperman's skepticism to work with while she had her feminine instincts. Whenever she ignored them, she was almost always sorry.

"It will be all right," she assured him. "No one will be looking for Diane here."

"At the moment, I'm not as worried about who's looking for her as I am about who she's talking to." He stuffed his hands in his trouser pockets and rocked on his heels.

"Anne Marie is her mother. How can you believe she wouldn't have her best interests at heart? Besides, you didn't talk to her. I did. She wouldn't hurt Diane." She hoped. No, she was sure of it, and she'd appreciate it if he'd stop planting doubts in her head.

"Maybe not intentionally," he conceded. "I'd feel better if Diane would lie low until we really know what's going on."

"She's about as low as she can get. The girls are going bonkers, staying cooped up like they've been. I had to go out and buy them Cake."

"Cake? I saw a big container of Dee Dee's cookies in the cabinet. Have they gone through all of them already?"

Jennifer rolled her eyes. "I think you and I need to start listening to some new radio stations. Hear anything from the police?"

"They're following the drug angle. Seems there were some narcotics taken that night at the clinic."

"A few moments passed after they shot Johnny and before they came looking for us. Maybe they were setting up a cover by grabbing a few painkillers."

"Could be. If those creeps in the alley were actually looking for drugs, I can't help but wonder why they'd hit the place so early—before eleven o'clock—rather than waiting until the middle of the night. And there's always my original question: Why that place?"

"Could have been the first in a series," Jennifer suggested.

"I haven't heard of any other break-ins at medical facilities." He shrugged. "The police can't seem to come up with another motive, so they're going after what they have."

"Did you talk with Wayne Hoffman?"

"Yeah. Decent guy. Devastated by his wife's death. Seems like he was totally devoted to her."

"So, did he have any idea who might have killed her?"

"Nah. He didn't even know she was going to the clinic that night. Gave him some story about taking in a late movie with a friend. He'd fallen asleep on the couch watching some crime show. He didn't even stir until a couple of policemen showed up banging on his door and told him she was dead."

"Home. Alone. No alibi."

"Except for the kids sleeping upstairs," Sam said. He raised an eyebrow at her. "You think he got himself a buddy and a truck, showed up in the alley, killed his wife, and then searched Diane's dorm room and broke into your apartment just to throw us off track?"

She glared at him. She hated it when he was so logical. "Even I know that when a spouse dies, the other spouse is *always* the first suspect. Besides, we still haven't actually established a link between Beverly's death and what happened at my apartment or Diane's dorm room."

"Okay, we won't cross him off. But I did ask around. The neighbors seem to think they were a loving couple, nice family, and everybody I talked with—including acquaintances, family, coworkers—really liked Beverly."

A little obvious hate about now might be helpful.

"Did those colleagues include any of the doctors at the clinic?"

"Yeah. McEvoy. He struck me as kind of a cold fish, more the scientist than Mr. Congeniality."

"What'd he have to say?"

"That she was a good nurse, but I had the impression he thought she was a little overly involved in her patients' lives. Too emotional to make good judgment calls."

"How can a nurse be too involved?" Jennifer asked.

"She had plans to go back to school, so she could counsel prospective patients, particularly surrogates."

"And he didn't approve?"

"Let's just say he questioned her judgment."

"How so?"

"When I mentioned his attitude to one of the other nurses, she said she thought it was because he didn't want the clinic covering Beverly's tuition costs. But it was in her original contract when she came to work for them, so he couldn't block it. Sweet deal."

Maybe not sweet enough.

"Did you get a chance to speak with Sullivan?" she asked.

"Oh, yeah. The iron lady. Made it through med school back when lady docs weren't popular. Kind of liked her, but I wouldn't want to cross her. She seems to be one of those women with all the answers. Easy to get along with as long as you agree with her."

"What happens if you don't?"

"I don't intend to find out."

She nodded. She'd met the type. Had one in charge of her writers' group.

"Hoffman seemed awfully chummy with the Colliers at the funeral," she said.

"Family helping family."

It'd be nice if it were always that simple.

"And Beverly had only the two children?" she asked casually.

"A four-year-old girl and a nine-year-old boy."

"Not three?"

"What are you getting at? I think her husband would notice how many children they had."

"But you didn't ask him outright if there might be a third?" She grimaced. Even to her that sounded a little weird. "Look. Here's the deal. I saw the Colliers' older son, the one who was at the funeral, at last night's Wednesday church supper."

"Since when did you start going to church on Wednesday nights?"

She swatted at him. "You never saw Beverly, did you, that is, not while she was alive?"

He wrinkled his brow at her and shook his head.

"The Colliers couldn't have children of their own. That's why they opened the clinic. And now they have six. Only while I'm thinking they worked their magic in petri dishes, they must, at least for one of their children, have used a far easier, older method. Dee Dee told me they used every procedure available. But I hadn't—"

"What are you talking about?"

"Beverly was a surrogate. She had to be. It had to be her egg and whose sperm? Paul's? That kind of condition . . . Certainly none of the rest of them have it. It must come down in a direct line—"

"What are you getting at, assuming you're actually getting at something?"

She had to remind herself again why she kept him around.

"Let's just say Beverly Hoffman had the most unusual eyes I've ever seen—until last night."

"So?"

"Her son. He has her eyes," Jennifer said.

Chapter 23

"Her eyes?" Sam repeated. "What was so special about Beverly Hoffman's eyes?"

"It's called heterochromia. Each iris is a different color. I looked it up on the Internet last night after you'd gone to bed. It's not usually a recessive characteristic," she explained.

"Yeah, but they are family, aunt and niece. What are you implying?"

She wasn't implying anything. She thought she'd been saying it straight out. Beverly was the birth mother of one of the Colliers' sons. "Beverly Hoffman must have been a surrogate. She must have conceived and carried that child to term and then turned it over to them. Why would they have asked her to do that?"

Bearing a child, especially if it wasn't her own, for someone else was nothing to be taken lightly. She'd followed April's first pregnancy from leg cramps to edema to not being able to tie her shoes, until the night of one writers' meeting when April, rounded to the point of a beached whale, announced she'd had it. That baby could get himself born immediately or find himself another mother. She wasn't carrying around that freeloader one minute longer. It was either him or her. One of them had to have some relief.

It didn't help that she was scared. Or that Leigh Ann

kept assuring her how natural the process was—as if she knew anything about it. Or that Teri insisted that women had been doing it for millions of years so what was the big deal. Of course, that only applied to other people, not to Teri herself, who wanted none of it. Ever.

The enormity, both physically and mentally, of the whole birthing process had been almost more than April could deal with. She couldn't seem to come to terms with the idea that a human being was actually growing inside her, and that she was a part of that miracle.

And now, with the second one, it seemed more like a been-there-done-that kind of thing. She didn't talk about it much. Still, if she could have gotten the kid by mail order, she would have done it in a heartbeat—an option Jennifer wouldn't mind having herself.

And that's why part of the selection criteria for surrogate mothers was that they already have children of their own. And that they were older than the early twenties that Beverly Hoffman had to have been when she gave birth. Jennifer knew all about it. She watched all the TV magazine news shows.

So, what had happened in this case?

"Women do it all the time," Sam assured her, as though he had a clue what he was talking about. Having babies was the one thing Sam could be sure he'd never be asked to do. "She was probably close to her aunt. They must have trusted her."

Sure. That explained the Colliers' motives. It didn't explain why a young woman, recently married, childless, would agree to such an arrangement. Had they offered her money?

"How long did you say Beverly had worked at the clinic?"

"About sixteen years. She started fresh out of school with her B.S. in nursing."

So she'd gone for training right after the child was born. And she was getting ready to go to graduate school with the clinic footing the bill. Was all of this coincidence or had Beverly gotten her education in return? And was that why Beverly had been so interested in screening surrogates—to make sure that what had happened to her didn't happen to anyone else?

Diane emerged from the tunnel followed closely by her mother. Neither of them was smiling.

"So how'd it go?" Jennifer asked, hoping it was better than it looked.

"She wants me to come home with her," Diane said, pulling her jacket closer over her chest.

"I think it'd be best," Anne Marie explained.

"There's a risk—" Sam began.

"There's a bigger risk if she stays here," Anne Marie insisted.

Diane threw up her hands. "Stop it! I'm not going anywhere. In two months I'll be eighteen. What are you going to do then? Boss me around? Tell me where I can go and with whom? You're not—"

Jennifer held her breath, watching Diane's chest heave, and prayed she wouldn't say what was on her lips.

"Mom, I have to do this. I need to find out what's going on here. You said you don't know. If that's true, you have to understand why I have to stay."

"Okay, okay." Anne Marie had her own demons to overcome, and one of them was allowing her daughter to choose how to protect herself. "I'll stay at the motel. You can reach me there if you need me." She threw a pleading glance in Jennifer's direction. "I don't suppose you'd at least give me a phone number."

"We'll call. I promise."

Anne Marie hugged her daughter, but Diane's only participation was to allow it to happen. Mrs. Robbins turned and headed back up the sidewalk toward the parking lot.

Jennifer caught up with her. "One question," she said as she kept up the brisk pace. "The birth date on the birth certificate. Is it the day Diane celebrates as her birthday?"

"Of course, November the first. Why?"

"No reason. I'll be in touch."

Jennifer stopped walking. Anne Marie took two more steps before she stopped and turned to Jennifer. "Thank you," she said, coming back to her and briefly squeezing her hand. Then she hurried toward her car.

Jennifer watched as the woman found her Chevy Suburban and climbed into it. She seemed exactly what she purported to be, a nice person who wanted only one thing in life: to have children and raise them. She certainly didn't look like someone who would buy a baby.

Chapter 24

Monique could bully a bouncer. She tossed back the five pages of medical history, complete with clipboard, that the nurse insisted she fill out and demanded to speak with the doctor immediately.

"I have no intention of providing you with personal information before I've interviewed your director and inspected your facilities. If I decide at that time that I intend to use your services, I will provide you with what data I deem necessary. Do we understand one another?"

Jennifer stared up at the nurse from under her lashes, consciously suppressing a grin. She'd been on the receiving end of Monique's barrages often enough to know that the poor nurse didn't stand a chance. Monique Dupree had spoken.

The nurse backed off, clutching the clipboard to her chest. "If you'll review the literature I've given you—"

Monique shoved the printed folders into Jennifer's hands. "I don't intend to spend my time reading your materials when I have a few simple questions that you no doubt have failed to cover."

The nurse was trying hard to keep her cool. "All right, then. We'll have a room ready for you—"

"No room," Monique told her.

"But I thought—"

"The doctor can see me in his office."

It wasn't a request.

"I'll see what—" the nurse stammered.

"You do that."

The woman backed away, and Teri tugged on Jennifer's sleeve. "What'd I tell you? Monique—"

"You two hush," Monique warned, obviously ready to put each of them in her place if need be. She was on, and she wasn't about to let anybody spoil her performance. They settled back in their chairs and waited. Neither Teri nor Jennifer dared utter a word. At least they didn't have to wait long. The nurse was back in less than five minutes.

"Mrs. DeWinter, Dr. Collier will see you now."

She led them to a nicely decorated office with built-in bookcases and walls warmed with paneled wood from the chair rail down. It looked more like a private library than anything else. The younger Dr. Collier was seated behind a large desk, wearing a white shirt and dark tie beneath his white medical jacket.

Darn. They'd been counting on meeting Paul. He was the sleazy one, if looks were any indication, and the one Jennifer pegged as the ringleader.

Donald rose and greeted them as they entered, offering his hand. "Mrs. DeWinter, so nice to meet you. And these are your . . ." he said, indicating Jennifer and Teri. He stopped short of saying family. They were living in the new South, and while the races mixed every day, it was never wise to assume.

"My niece," Monique explained, nodding in Jennifer's direction, "and my nanny for when the baby comes."

If Teri was irritated, she kept it to herself. She was about as unlikely a candidate for child care as they came. Rugrats, she called them.

"Please have a seat," he said, indicating chairs and then taking his own seat.

"I had expected to see Dr. Paul Collier," Monique insisted.

"That Dr. Collier is not in right now, but I'll be more than glad to help you. Now if—"

"But I was assured when I called—"

"Mrs. DeWinter, I'm sorry. He's already gone home for the day. We worked you in when you didn't have an appointment," he reminded her. "Now what can I do for you? I believe my nurse gave you all the literature we have about our procedures. Our candidates undergo an extensive screening process. We don't deal with false hopes here. We'll tell you right away if we can help you or not."

"Good. That's exactly what I want you to do," Monique declared. "I've been to some of the best clinics in the country, Dr. Collier. I can't have children. You don't have a procedure that will help me, and even if you did, I wouldn't care to put myself through it. Not again."

He looked surprised and a little confused. "I see, then why—"

"My husband and I have decided enough is enough. I want a baby. The normal avenues are closed to us because of our age—"

"And how old would that be?"

"Fifty-five."

She'd upped her age by at least ten and maybe fifteen years. Go, Monique! This woman had no vanity when it came to getting the job done.

"I would never have thought—"

"Thank you."

She actually looked gracious. Monique was good at this, really good.

"As I was saying, I want a baby. I want to adopt, but I will not go through a private adoption. We've tried that before only to have the birth mother back out when the baby was born. As I've said, the public sector is of no help. Money is not an issue, Dr. Collier. Can you help me?"

He looked confused. "Mrs. DeWinter, I certainly sympathize with your desire for a family, but we are a fertility clinic. I'm a little puzzled as to why you would come to us. We don't deal with adoptions."

"I understand the position I'm putting you in, Dr. Collier." She leaned in close and searched his face with such sincerity that Jennifer almost believed her herself. "I don't ask this of you lightly. But, surely, being in the business you're in, you must occasionally come across a situation where a child is not . . . um . . . wanted. Any arrangements we make will be held in the strictest confidence. I'm very wealthy, Dr. Collier, and I'm prepared to wait a reasonable amount of time if that's what it takes."

"Are you suggesting—"

Monique shook her head and feigned innocence. "I'm not suggesting anything. I have only one question for you: Can you help me?"

"The very newest procedures involve fertilizing donated eggs with donated sperm and implanting them in a surrogate. We haven't actually done one at this clinic, but only because no one has asked us before. It'd be quite expensive, and, I'm afraid, potentially a legal nightmare. It would help a great deal if the child were biologically linked in some way to either your husband or yourself, as protection should a custody battle ensue."

"Sort of a made-to-order kid," Teri piped up.

Collier turned toward her and smiled, but without much humor. "Not quite. We don't do gene manipulations. You can't order, say, red hair and brown eyes. Not yet, at least. Not here."

"I don't suppose you have one ready-made?" Teri asked.

Collier gave her an odd look.

Monique was immediately on her feet. "Thank you, Doctor."

"Shall I have the nurse set up the initial appointments?"

"Not yet. I'll call the office after I've talked it over with my husband."

"Certainly. It would be an interesting case. I hope to be working with you soon."

They couldn't get out of the office fast enough.

"It boggles the mind," Jennifer said, still reeling from their interview with Collier. She was living in a brave new world and hadn't even realized it. She leaned her head forward between the bucket seats of Monique's coupé. "You can actually go into that clinic and place an order for a baby."

"Not exactly the black market we were looking for," Teri pointed out. "I mean, why would they bother stealing babies when they can mix one up in their lab for anyone willing to pay the price?"

"Good question," Monique agreed. "But that kind of technology wasn't available when Diane was born. Which means they may have been in the business back then even if they aren't now."

"Right," Jennifer said. "We know for a fact that Paul Collier gave a child to Anne Marie Robbins. And once she held Diane in her arms, Paul knew she'd do anything for that child. If you'd only heard her tell it."

"So how much did he get for her?" Teri asked.

"I don't know." It made her sick to think about money actually exchanging hands. "She's never mentioned money."

"Find out," Monique said. "If we can trace the payment, we'll have them."

Sure. That shouldn't be a problem. Assuming they had the FBI on their side.

Chapter 25

Jennifer had cut Johnny Z enough slack to wrap himself in it twice. Now it was time for him to come clean, to do some sharing of his own. After all, she was aiding and abetting him. If she went down for it, she'd like to have a clue what it was they'd done.

She'd practically stolen that deposit slip out of Mrs. Robbins' purse. Okay. So she had an overactive conscience. But she still felt a duty to make sure he didn't misuse the information. And if he were looking into the Robbinses' finances, maybe he'd found a withdrawal, say in the amount needed to buy a baby. Whatever that was.

"You done good, doll," Johnny told her, stretched back in his swivel desk chair, his hands behind his head. He looked his emaciated best and just a little too pleased with the fact she'd come looking for him late on a Friday morning.

The office was a mess, as usual, so she chose to stand.

"You come to take me up on that lunch?"

"Cut to the chase, Johnny," she warned. "What's the word on the Robbinses' finances?"

"It's amazing what you can find out with a few numbers," he told her, obviously in no hurry to get to the point. "People should treat their numbers with more respect. You get them, you got a record of their whole life."

"Okay, I can tell you found something. Tell me. Or do I have to give you one of those little gold stars first?"

"Marsh, you cut me to the quick. Here I am, ready to share with you, and you put me down. You should be singing my praises."

"Fine. Give me an idea what the first verse should be about."

He slid forward in his chair, rubbed his craggy face, and then crossed his hands. "Fortunately for us, when Robbins moved north, he transferred his account rather than closing the old one and opening a new one. Makes it easier to do a little checking. He's self-employed, which means he's got money coming into and going out of that account in no particular order or amount except for the standard monthly bills—mortgage, utilities, etcetera. Only there's this one deposit like clockwork. Five grand shows up every August the fourteenth, every year since they made the move to Smith Mountain fourteen years ago."

"So what's the significance of that date?"

"Damned if I know."

"Could you trace where the money came from? Do you know who wrote the check?"

"No checks. Cash deposits, most likely in an overnight depository."

"So who were they blackmailing?" Jennifer asked, stunned by the idea of Anne Marie being mixed up in some nefarious activity. And she'd trusted the woman.

"Wait a minute, little lady. That's a major leap. Money passing hands don't always mean blackmail, you know."

Maxie Malone would have punched out anyone calling her 'little lady,' but at the moment Jennifer didn't much care. She was reeling from the idea that Diane's parents might not be the good guys. She sank into the vinyl and chrome armchair to the left of the desk. Dirt, at this point, was the least she had to worry about.

"How'd you know to look for it?" she asked.

"I didn't. I was expecting money going in the other direction. I figured this Collier might be putting the squeeze for a little cash now and then, but no deal. No big withdrawals other than moving expenses, and all of them are documented."

Whenever she thought she had even the vaguest notion of what was going on, things got curiouser and curiouser.

"There had to be a large withdrawal around the time Diane was adopted," Jennifer insisted.

He shook his head.

"So where'd the money come from to pay Collier?"

He started to chuckle, but it broke into a raspy cough. He cleared his throat. "You're making an assumption not in evidence. I'm telling you, money is going into Diane's family's account. Not out. Period."

She felt like shaking him. Any P.I. worth his salt should have been able to find a record of the cash.

"Is that it?" she asked, sitting up and more than ready to be out of that office.

"You act like I don't have nothin' to do but chase after this Robbins case."

"Well, do you?"

He shrugged. "Did check out the father. He's right where he's supposed to be, straightening out some computer glitches for an outfit in D.C. I don't think we have to worry about him."

Apparently nobody, including Mrs. Robbins, had bothered to notify Mr. Robbins. He seemed to be the forgotten man.

"One thing's still bugging me," Johnny confided.

"That nurse—Beverly Hoffman—she was gonna pass somethin' over to me that night. I'd kinda like to know who has it."

And so would she.

Chapter 26

One more day without her books, and Diane was going to be toast. She might as well die right then and there, in Sam's living room, because Lanier would expel her, her scholarship would be passed along to some more deserving freshman, her parents would disown her, and, heaven forbid, she'd never see Jared again.

Whoever Jared was.

So when she left Johnny's office, Jennifer headed over to Lanier to get the girls their books, some clean underwear, and Valerie's hair gel and dryer. If anybody followed her back to the apartment, she'd deal with them. Some things were worth the risk. Dodging bad guys couldn't possibly be any more difficult than two teenage girls without their strawberry body wash.

A smile, a lot of fast talk, and a note from Diane got her access to room 205 of James Hall on the north side of Lanier's small campus.

"Make sure you let me know when you leave, so I can check to see the room's locked up properly," the residence director, a first-year grad student, told her as she turned the key in the lock. It took both of them to push the door open all the way with all the clothing on the floor.

"Are Diane and Valerie all right?"

143

"Fine," Jennifer assured her, distracted by the unbelievable mess. Someone had thoroughly trashed the place. Either that or these girls were bigger slobs than she and her own roommate had ever been, which, unfortunately, was unlikely. It made the search of her apartment look like it had been conducted by a couple of Felix Ungers. Oscar Madison must have been the main man on this one.

"Pretty scary, huh?" the woman said.

Jennifer nodded.

"You come to clean it up?"

"Oh, no. I just hope to take the girls some of the necessities of life, assuming I can find them in here somewhere. You know, CDs, eyelash curlers, lip balm. And textbooks, of course. Diane's an Elliot Woodrow scholar."

"What's that?"

"Full tuition, room and board, plus expense money."

"Yeah? Well, that's a new one on me. I'd like to have had it when I was an undergrad here. The best they offered then was full tuition, and those were so competitive they were impossible to get."

She said it as if it had been long ago, but it couldn't have been more than a year, maybe two.

"Well, I'll leave you alone." The woman quickly backed out of the room, apparently afraid that if she stayed too long, Jennifer might ask for some help. And with good reason. She needed help.

She bent and scooped up the items directly in front of her, a pair of jeans and a sweatshirt, and tossed them toward the single bed to her right. It gave her enough room to step past the door and actually survey the room.

It was small, but large enough to house two single beds, two dressers, and two desks. Posters of heavy metal rock bands lined one wall, new age groups the other. Cutouts from magazines filled in every other inch of wall space. Books, papers, toiletries, a computer, stereo, and TV mushroomed from every flat surface.

"Hey! So you finally decided to—" The voice stopped, and Jennifer turned. He was about five-nine, thin, with an unbuttoned shirt, sleeves rolled to the elbows, over a T-shirt. His dark hair, parted in the middle, was tucked behind his ears. His upper lip sported a mustache and his chin what would have been a goatee if he could have grown it. In one hand was a Tootsie Roll Pop, and in the other a couple of envelopes.

He gave Jennifer the once-over and shrugged. "I saw the door open and thought Diane had come back." He stuck the pop into his mouth and then staggered back dramatically. "What the hell happened here?"

"Don't you know?" she asked.

He dropped the act. "Well, yeah. But I didn't get to see it before. Diane and Valerie cut out before I got back that night. I heard it was, like, trashed, but man . . ."

"Yeah, pretty scary stuff."

"So what'd this dude have against Diane?"

Jennifer looked at him. "Why Diane? Why not Valerie?"

He took the pop out of his mouth and pointed with it. "The dresser and the desk. And the bed. Those are Diane's."

He was right. Only one dresser had been tossed. And one desk. And one bed had its mattress pulled out. In the disorder, it was easy not to notice.

"So, you got a name?" Jennifer asked.

He sucked hard on the candy as though sizing her up. "Jared."

She'd suspected as much. He looked like something that would appeal to Diane. "So, Jared, Diane tells me the two of you are friends."

"You a relative of hers or somethin'?"

She ignored the question, just as Johnny had taught her. "Tell me, what is it about Valerie you don't like?"

She was fishing, but he didn't know that. For all he knew, Diane had given her the lowdown on the whole floor.

He looked at her with dark, brooding eyes. "She's possessive."

Ah, yes. If she'd had any doubts before, they had vanished. Jared *was* the boyfriend.

He shifted, and she knew she was losing him.

"I gotta go."

"Don't forget to leave the mail."

She pointed at the envelopes in his hand. When she was in college, at any given time at least three other people knew the combination to her mailbox. She suspected Diane was no different.

"That's why you came by, wasn't it? You heard someone in the room, and you brought over the mail, right? I was planning to stop by the student union to pick it up, but since you've already done that . . ." She held out her hand.

He held up the envelopes and shook them in her direction, then let out a sigh and handed them over. "Tell her . . . Tell her . . ."

"Yes?" Jennifer said.

"Tell her I'll see her later."

She nodded and watched as he disappeared back into the hallway.

She had a lot of work to do before she could get out of there, but she couldn't help but sort through Diane's mail. Checking the mail was one of the big events of a writer's day, one she sorely missed.

She thumbed through the envelopes. Between what looked like a card from Anne Marie and a notice from the registrar's office was a business-size envelope with

Diane's name, Lanier College, Macon, Georgia, and a zip code scrawled across it. No box number. In the upper left-hand corner was printed the address of the East Lake Fertility Clinic. The postmark was dated the Monday after the murder.

Chapter 27

"Open it," Jennifer demanded, hovering over Diane.

She'd sent Valerie out to walk Muffy, so the two of them could be alone when she gave Diane her mail. Besides, Muffy was bursting to get out. She'd explored every nook and cranny of Sam's apartment and was up for adventure.

"Do you mind? You're taking up more than your share of oxygen," Diane declared.

Jennifer calmed herself and drew back. She was, after all, the adult here. But if Diane didn't open that envelope in the next thirty seconds, she couldn't be held responsible for her actions.

Diane sat in Sam's one good chair, running her hands over the paper's edge. "What if it's—"

Jennifer gave her a dangerous look from her perch on the arm.

"All right already." Diane slipped her finger under the seal and loosened the flap. Then she took a deep breath and pulled out what was inside, a thin piece of cardboard with a flat, metal disk Scotch-taped to it. She opened the envelope wide and shook it, but it was empty.

She looked at it and then asked, "What's this?"

Jennifer examined the engraving. It read, *CAT's cat.* "It looks like one of those pet ID tags you attach to a collar. Muffy has one. In case she gets lost, whoever finds her can call me. Do you remember having a cat?"

Diane shook her head. "Only a little pink stuffed one that I've had forever."

"And what do you call it?"

Diane looked at her sheepishly. "Cat. I don't think it ever had another name."

She loosened the tape and lifted the shiny, silver tag. On the back was a hyphenated, seven digit number. "See?" Jennifer said.

"Yeah. But what's it got to do with anything, and how come I got it in the mail? Why would someone at the clinic be sending it to me?"

Excellent question, and one that sent Jennifer's mind clicking into overdrive. She felt sure they could assume they currently had no friends at the East Lake Fertility Clinic. Which meant . . . She stood and paced back and forth as goose bumps skittered up and down her arms.

"Let's say you're Beverly Hoffman. You're at the office late on a Sunday night. Nobody else is around, and you're waiting to pass some information to a private eye. Only you're early, and he hasn't shown up yet. You're getting nervous. You've put the information in an envelope. And then you hear something outside, only it's not what you expect to hear. It sounds like a truck, and you specifically told Zeeman to park at the end of the alley and walk up. You get worried. Then you start to panic. The last thing you need is someone coming in that clinic and finding you with whatever it is that you have. How are you going to get rid of it?"

"Is this how you plot your books? You get all red in the face and start acting it out in your mind?"

"I should have thought of this before. I mean it's a classic," Jennifer went on, totally ignoring Diane.

"What? The letter was addressed to me. *You* are

working for *me*, technically at least, even if I'm not paying you. So, would you like to tell—"

It was so simple. It should have been the first thing she thought of. "Ever read Edgar Allan Poe's 'The Purloined Letter'?"

Diane shook her head.

"Okay, forget that, but don't you see? That must have been what Beverly did. She must've hidden the envelope by putting it where letters go, in the Out box at the clinic before going to check who was at the back door. Only the people looking for it didn't know what they were looking for. They didn't think to go through the mail. And the next morning it went through the meter with all the rest of the envelopes. The office clerk wouldn't have questioned it. Lab reports and correspondence must go out all the time."

Diane looked at her as if she were nuts. "You mean *this* is what Hoffman was going to give me? This little piece of metal?"

She threw herself back into the chair in a major pout.

"This little piece of metal," Jennifer declared far more confidently than she felt, "may be the key to who you are. If Hoffman were somehow involved with your adoption—for lack of a better word—she could well have been in charge of removing any identifying information such as clothing labels, jewelry, whatever, that you might have had. And it's just possible that little stuffed cat of yours had a collar with this tag on it."

"Maybe. But why would she have kept it all these years?"

"Why not? She may have been afraid to throw it away. It won't burn, and it won't decay. Do you recognize the phone number?"

Diane took back the disk, looked at the numbers again, and shook her head.

The girl couldn't remember her name. It was unreasonable to think she could remember anything else.

"Get the phone book," Jennifer told her. "I think it's in a drawer in the kitchen. I'll find the atlas. I'm sure Sam has one somewhere, probably on that bookcase over there."

"Okay, fine, but what are we doing?" Diane asked.

"Finding out where you came from."

"This time you've lost it," Diane declared, abandoning all pretense at politeness. "Even if that were my phone number, as you seem to think, no way would it still be in operation, unless you think my real parents—" Her eyes grew wide, and Jennifer put a hand over Diane's.

"No, I don't. All I'm trying to do is find out what state and city you might have come from. I don't expect to find your parents, and neither should you."

She couldn't let herself or Diane think that, to hope that it might be as simple as dialing a phone number. Besides, what she had in mind was a long shot, at best. Those three missing girls on the net. One was from Philadelphia, one from Bethesda, Maryland, and one from Wilmington, North Carolina. A lot had changed in fourteen years. States had added area codes. But the exchanges had generally stayed the same. Even if Diane's parents no longer had that number—for whatever reason—it should ring through to the right area.

Diane brought the directory to the table, and Jennifer laid it side by side with the atlas. It looked like Philadelphia had a 215 area code, Bethesda 301, and Wilmington 252.

"There're fifty states," Diane reminded her. "What do you plan to do? Go through them one by one and ask if they've heard of . . . of who? A girl called Cat?"

"Indulge me for half a minute, will you?"

Diane glared back at her and opened her mouth.

But Jennifer shook her head. "That means shut up while I try something. If it doesn't work, then you can tell me how stupid I am."

She took up the phone, her heart beating in her ears, pressed 1, then 215, followed by the number on the tag. It rang. Then she heard a series of loud beeps. "Your call cannot be completed as dialed. Please hang up, check the number, and dial again," a recorded voice told her.

She hung up. Diane looked at her, and Jennifer shook her head. Then she tried the 301 code. A woman picked up. "Hello?" She sounded older.

"Excuse me," Jennifer said. "I was trying to reach the . . ." *Think fast, Jennifer. The woman can hang up on you any second.* ". . . the Barnes & Noble in Bethesda. Is this it?"

"I'm sorry. You've reached a private number."

She gave the woman the number she was dialing.

"That's my number, but—"

"So this is Bethesda? Bethesda, Maryland?"

"Yes."

"But I'm sure I copied it right. How long have you had it?" Mentally Jennifer crossed her fingers. Could this be one of Diane's relatives?

"Oh my. I'd say it's been a good six years. Ever since we moved here from—"

Darn.

"Thank you. Sorry to bother you." Jennifer dropped the receiver in its cradle. "That one's a maybe."

She dialed again, and it rang through. A man answered with "Mack's Grill."

"Where are you located?" Jennifer asked.

He gave her detailed directions, a little too detailed.

"I'm coming from Wilmington," she told him.

"Oh, then you're about forty-five minutes away. Come in on—"

"Thanks," she said, and hung up.

"That one's also a maybe, but a not likely."

"Three down and what? Forty-seven to go? Why aren't you calling numbers in Georgia?"

Because Georgia hadn't listed any missing three-year-olds that fit all of Diane's statistics. "As soon as I figure out—"

"Yeah, yeah, yeah." Diane curled up in a ball in the chair and turned away from her.

Her disappointment was understandable. Jennifer didn't know what she'd expected from Beverly Hoffman, but it was a lot more than a flat metal disk. It hardly seemed worth getting killed over.

A knock hit the door, and they could hear some familiar Muffy whimpers. Valerie was back.

Diane shoved off from the chair, but Jennifer stepped in her way. "Don't mention any of this to Valerie. Not the disk. Not the phone calls."

"Why?"

"Trust me," Jennifer insisted.

" 'Trust no one.' I learned that from *The X-Files*." She brushed past and unlocked the door.

Muffy nearly knocked them both down. She was soooo glad to see them.

But Diane said nothing, not to Valerie and not to Jennifer. She went back to the chair, drew up her legs, and pretended to go to sleep.

The computer screen glared in the darkness. The girls were both snuggled down in their sleeping bags, their breathing even and regular. Muffy lay next to her as Jennifer once again found the site for missing children. She skipped the one for Lori Jean Miller, the little girl from

Philadelphia, and clicked on the poster for Cynthia Allison Turner, last seen in Bethesda, Maryland.

Cynthia Allison Turner. She stared at that sweet little face. Round cheeks, baby nose, bright smile with tiny teeth, dark eyes, and a bow holding her wispy hair off her face. A beautiful child. If this were indeed Diane, the age-enhanced photo had left out one important element, something essential to make her recognizable. Attitude.

Cynthia Allison Turner. She whispered the name aloud to herself. And then her hands began to shake. Her stomach suddenly felt strangely hollow. It had gone right past her the first time. CAT. Initials. CAT, not Cat. Why hadn't she seen it?

Born August 14. If she'd had any doubt before, it was gone now. Five thousand dollars deposited yearly in the Robbinses' bank account on CAT's birthday. Coincidence? She hardly thought so.

But here was the kicker, the really bad part, the reason Jennifer had hoped that if Diane were one of the three, she wouldn't be Cynthia: *Not found at crime scene of parents' murder/suicide.*

Chapter 28

"Can't this wait until morning?" Sam insisted, groggy and grouchy both. Most unattractive. Although he did look cute in his T-shirt and sweatpants, no doubt a concession to having ladies in the house.

"What's so important you have to wake me out of a sound sleep and drag me into the bathroom at . . ." He looked at his watch. "Good grief! Do you realize it's almost one in the morning?"

"But you don't understand. I know who Diane is," Jennifer told him in a loud whisper, bouncing on her heels. She couldn't wait till morning. She couldn't wait another minute.

He shook his head as if to clear it. "Come again?"

"Diane is Cynthia Allison Turner. C-A-T. It was initials. Not short for Catherine or Caitlin or anything. 'Cat.' All caps." She'd backed him up against the sink and was leaning forward. She was invading his space, but she couldn't help it. The bathroom was only so big. Her news was bigger.

He put his arms around her, resting them on her hips, but she broke away. She would have paced, but she had only three feet of floor space to work with.

"It all fits. Her birthday is August fourteenth, not November first. The deposits made into her parents' accounts were always on that date."

"What deposits?"

That's right. He didn't know anything about what Johnny had found out. So she told him, about that and the pet ID that had come in the mail, about making the phone calls and looking up everything on the Internet.

That woke him up.

"What have you told Diane?" he asked.

"Nothing yet."

"Good."

"What do you mean?"

"I think it's premature. If other children came through the clinic like you've been suggesting all along, who's to say the tag didn't belong to one of them? You don't even know for sure it's what Beverly Hoffman had to give you. Or that she actually knew who Diane is."

He was good at bringing her down.

"And the phone call? How do you explain that?" she asked, some of her confidence returning.

"It rang through. So what? I bet if you tried a dozen or more area codes, you'd have a dozen or more possibilities for where that number was from."

"But what about 'Cat'?"

"It could still be short for Catherine or some other name. Or a pet name. It's not all that unusual." He took her by the shoulders. "The truth is we still don't know. Not for sure."

Every instinct she had was telling her she was right. "But . . ." She waited for him to interrupt, only he didn't. "So you think I should forget about it?"

As if she would.

"Of course not. I'm saying let's check it out first, find out what the story is with the Turners, how and why they died. If—and please note the *if*—we can find a link between them and the clinic, then we may have something."

It was like Cinderella going to the ball. If she scrubbed the floors and beat the rugs, if she . . . but he was right. They couldn't tell Diane what she'd found without more proof. It would be devastating. She was just getting used to the idea she was adopted. They could hardly add, "By the way, we think your natural parents may have died in a murder/suicide." At least not until they were sure. Diane was fragile, even if she didn't act like it. What's more, she trusted them. Jennifer wanted to keep that trust.

"Okay, so where do we go from here?" she asked.

"I'd vote for back to bed."

He nuzzled her neck. She would have swatted him, but he'd probably yelp and wake up the girls. And that's why she'd dragged him into the bathroom in the first place, so Diane and Valerie wouldn't know what was going on.

"Quit it!" she ordered, pulling his face up nose-to-nose with her own. She had to avoid those eyes. They'd be her undoing yet. So she looked at his mouth. Another not-so-safe area. Maybe if she concentrated on the stubble on his chin . . .

But she didn't have to. He turned his back on her and splashed water all over his face. She handed him a hand towel from the rack behind her, and he ran it over his skin.

"Tell you what," he said, turning back. "First thing Monday morning, I'll get in touch with—you said it was in Maryland?"

"Bethesda. Montgomery County."

"Right. And I'll see what they're willing to tell me. Then we'll decide whether or not I need to go up there."

"We," she said.

"We who?"

"We, as in you and me. Whether or not *we* need to go up there."

"What would we do with the girls?"

"Dee Dee has a spare room."

"You want to bring her into this?"

Not really.

"Anne Marie, then," she suggested. "She's staying at the Residence Inn. I'm sure she has room for two more, at least for a day or so. Besides, surely if *they* were going to try something, they would have done it by now. The first few days, I kept waiting for the other shoe to drop, for someone to find us, break in, at least search the place. But now . . ."

"Yeah, me, too," Sam agreed. "Doesn't mean Diane's safe. Sometimes danger simply takes another form."

Great. Just what she needed: a morphing threat. It'd be nice if for once Sam would tell her what she wanted to hear. Even if it wasn't true.

"Could you at least call the police in the morning?" she asked.

"On a Saturday? We want their cooperation, not their wrath. This is an old case. If this child's been missing for fourteen years, I doubt they'll think we constitute an emergency. We can wait two days. We don't exactly have a smoking gun."

It had looked smoking to her, right up until he threw cold water on it.

"Okay. Monday morning, then." She turned to him. "Sam?"

He yawned. "Yeah?"

"Thanks."

He blinked and raised an eyebrow at her as if he felt sure there was a catch. "For . . ."

"For taking Muffy and me in. For putting up with Diane and Valerie. For letting us take over your place and disrupt your life. For buying ice cream."

He nodded and one side of his mouth curled upward.

"It hasn't been quite what I'd had in mind when I brought you home."

She put a finger over his lips. It wasn't wise to go there. Moments pass. Whatever might have been was long gone.

He blew out a puff of air through his nose, shook his head, and hugged her tight. "Sometimes you're more trouble than you could possibly be worth."

She shrugged in his embrace. "I know."

Chapter 29

Calling a person a leech was not nice. Sam should be ashamed of himself. Besides, no one—except Sam—seemed to mind having her at the *Telegraph* offices. She was quietly minding her own business, perched on the front edge of his desk, waiting for him to finish his phone call to Bethesda. Besides, who was awake enough at eight-thirty in the morning to notice her?

Finally, he hung up. "Do you mind?" he asked, obviously irritated. "You didn't have to come down with me. I told you I'd call you when I had something." He looked around the office and added, "It's hard for me to pretend to be working when you're sitting on my desk like a hood ornament."

She stood up, pulling down her short skirt. "My. Aren't we testy this morning."

"Could be from lack of sleep this weekend."

And could be from what he learned, or more likely, didn't learn, in that phone call. "Want to share?"

"Only if you'll agree to go home and let me work."

"I can live with that."

Sam took up his notes. "I spoke with Detective Lou Myers of the Montgomery County police. Robert Turner and his wife, Colette, were found dead at their residence after a neighbor reported hearing gunshots at their home in the late evening hours. When police arrived, they found what appeared to be a murder/suicide with Robert having shot Colette and then turning the gun on himself. The child was discovered missing only after a relative, Mrs. Turner's mother, was informed, and she asked about her. Myers repeated the information you'd already learned over the Internet, the description of the child and so forth. And that's all he would tell me over the phone. He said he might be able to make some time to see me early next week if I wanted to fly up."

She harumphed. "That wasn't worth the price of the phone call."

"I'll get in touch with Tim Donahue and see if he can find out anything else. And I'll check the library. Maybe they have copies of *The Washington Post* on microfiche that might have carried stories about the murder."

"That's a major newspaper. Why would they carry it?"

"Bethesda is close to D.C. Some people would call it a suburb, although I expect the people who live there wouldn't appreciate it."

"And they'd run stories like that?"

"Sure. Actually, it would be local news. The infamous Beltway around D.C. runs across northern Virginia and circles on around through Montgomery and Prince Georges counties in Maryland. Doesn't even touch the D.C. line. Bethesda's inside the Beltway, right on the D.C. border."

"So the nearest airport would be . . ."

"Reagan National in Arlington."

"Fine," she said, and turned to leave.

"Where ya going?" he asked.

"To find a way to finance a trip to Maryland," she called over her shoulder. "I know you don't have the money, and I certainly don't." She suspected that was why he wasn't so hot to take off up north in the first place. He didn't get paid until next week.

"Jennifer . . ." he said, with that warning tone in his voice.

At the door she turned back and blew him a kiss. He looked none too happy. He could talk to Donahue if he wanted to, he could even fly to the moon, for all she cared, but she wanted answers. Now. And she intended to get them.

Johnny had to be in there. He wasn't at his office, even if the hours on the door did read nine to five. She continued to hammer the door of the condo a few blocks off the downtown part of Riverside. It wasn't one of the more affluent areas of Macon, but it looked like someplace Johnny would choose to live.

After several minutes he jerked open the door, rubbing his eyes and squinting in the light. He had on a pair of dress trousers, no belt, and a T-shirt that barely covered the bandage on his chest.

"Oh, it's you." He turned and walked away without another word, leaving the door open. She took that as an invitation to come in, closing the door after her. When she turned around, he'd disappeared into the darkness. Sounds of running water came from the hallway.

She opened the blinds over the sink. It was a kitchen/ living room combination, with a breakfast bar marking where one ended and the other began. She looked around. The kitchen tile had chipped, leaving black patches of tar to peek through, and the bright, mustard-colored Formica on the countertops had several burn marks on it. She turned to the stove and lifted the lid of a pot that held the remains of what must have been last night's dinner, some kind of tuna noodle mixture. Yuck.

After a minute or two Johnny emerged from the hallway, running a towel across his face which he then draped over one shoulder as he joined her near the sink.

He must have been drinking the night before because the light from the window made him wince. He reached up and tilted the blinds to reduce the glare. If she'd had a cigarette, she would have offered it to him. He looked like he was in the final stages of nicotine withdrawal.

"You want some coffee?" he offered, holding a pot half filled with dark liquid in her direction.

She started to answer, but he'd already turned his back on her, dumped it in the sink, and was refilling it with water. When he turned back, he had a cigarette hanging from his lips. Must keep them where most people keep soap. She hoped none of the ash had fallen into the pot. Not that she planned to drink any of that coffee anyway.

Johnny pulled the coffee tin out of the freezer and filled the basket, then turned on the coffee maker and leaned back against the counter. He looked more or less awake, although he still couldn't quite get his eyes open. He yawned, one of those puff-out-the-belly yawns. "So what's up, doll? I'm sure you didn't get me out of bed at the crack of dawn to tell me you love me."

"It's ten-thirty, and no, I didn't."

She handed him the disk along with a printout of the information she'd found on the Internet.

He rubbed his eyes with the heel of the hand that held his cigarette and then shoved it back at her. "Just fill me in. I don't focus so good this early in the morning."

She told him about Robert and Colette Turner. "Diane needs to know. Is it them?"

He seemed to be studying her. Or maybe he was simply thinking.

"Sam says we need a link between the Turners and the clinic," she went on.

"You been talkin' to Sam about this case?" he asked.

"Diane *is* living at his place—where *you* sent her," she reminded him. "Look. Here's the problem: we don't know how or why a three-year-old could have gotten from Bethesda, Maryland, to Macon, Georgia. I say we go there. Check it out in person. It's more complicated than the police think it is. This isn't a matter of a child wandering off somewhere. The child wound up over seven hundred miles away from the crime scene."

"Assuming Diane is Cat Turner."

What was it with these guys? Why couldn't they cope with a tiny leap of logic?

Johnny continued to stare at her and draw on his cigarette. Then he took her by the elbow and shuffled her toward the door. "Go home," he said. "I got somethin' to check out."

"No," Jennifer said, pulling back out of his grip and turning to face him. "You said we were partners. True or not, I want to know—"

"I'll call you," he said, pushing her out the door and pulling it shut, right in her face.

She stood there, blinking at the wood. Fine, then. If Sam was spinning his wheels, and Johnny didn't have time for her, she'd take care of it without them. And she knew exactly who would be willing to help her.

Chapter 30

"I know you didn't hire our firm," Jennifer told Anne Marie, playing with a napkin that was tucked into a stemmed glass, as she balanced on a stool in Unit 207 at the Residence Inn. "But your daughter did, and the only way I see that we can break this case is to fly to Maryland. Immediately."

Anne Marie turned the shiny disk over in her hand. "Maryland," she repeated as though it were a foreign country. She sank onto a stool next to Jennifer.

"Have you seen the disk before?" Jennifer asked.

The woman shook her head. "She had a little, pink stuffed cat when we got her. It had a collar on it, a real one, like you would buy in a pet store. Did she tell you?"

Jennifer nodded.

"It was her only possession. She clung to it. Wouldn't let anybody take it from her, not even when she took a bath. I had to put it in a Baggie right up to its neck. She wouldn't let me cover its head. Said it had to be able to breathe."

She looked up at Jennifer. "So you think her parents are dead?"

"Yeah, I do. She doesn't know."

"Good. Don't tell her until you're sure. And please, please let me be there."

"Of course," Jennifer assured her. What she really

wanted to do was walk away from this whole situation. Tell Diane to go home with her mother and be thankful for her blessings. Let the past stay buried. But until they knew why Hoffman was killed, Diane could never have a normal life.

"I hate to ask you," Jennifer began. She hated money altogether, but it was a necessary evil. And she hated asking anyone for it even when she was doing them a service. Still, she had to be realistic. She wasn't getting to Maryland without it. "We don't have any operating funds. Diane didn't give us a retainer, and—"

"Fine," Anne Marie said, slipping off the stool and heading for the bedroom. She was back in no time with her purse and her checkbook.

"How much do you need?"

"I'm not sure. Round trip airfare for three, money for expenses . . ."

"Will five thousand be enough?" Anne Marie asked, writing out the check without giving Jennifer an opportunity to answer.

Jennifer swallowed hard. The Robbinses had had their yearly bonus deposited on August 14. It seemed ironic that she was being offered that money, in effect, to find out who had been making those very deposits.

She took the check. It had been made out to "The Johnny Zeeman Detective Agency." Crumb. That meant she'd have to get Johnny to cash it. But she couldn't very well ask the woman to void it and make out another to her personally. And she certainly didn't have the authority to take money on her own.

She slipped off the stool, and Anne Marie walked her to the door. "The girls still don't feel safe going back to campus. While we're gone, could they stay . . ."

For the first time since she'd met her, Anne Marie smiled.

Chapter 31

Thank God for her Monday night writers' group! It gave her something to do while waiting for Johnny Z to finally get in touch with her. He had to endorse that check before she could make the plane reservations. She'd left messages at his house and at his office, and still nothing.

She'd waited past the time she usually left for group. And Sam hadn't shown either. Diane and Valerie moped through their homemade macaroni and cheese and Caesar's salad. They liked it better when Sam cooked. He fixed beef.

At least now that she was at Monique's, she could momentarily shelve Diane's problems and find her center again. It seemed like her own life had gotten lost in the shuffle. Diane dominated her every waking thought. And she wasn't the only one. Valerie, Anne Marie, Sam, even Johnny, seemed so tangled in this mess, none of them could function normally. Well, surely by the time she got home she would have heard something.

She glanced at her watch. It was a full twenty minutes after seven, and they were still waiting on April.

They heard a bump at the door. Leigh Ann jumped up to get it. April, her hair uncombed, waddled in straight to the couch.

167

"Sorry," she declared, bracing herself on the sofa arm and lowering herself carefully onto the cushion.

"You all right?" Jennifer asked, noting that April hadn't brought a single snack bag. Something was definitely amiss.

April nodded distractedly. "Go ahead. I'm sorry I made you all wait."

"That's all right," Monique assured her. "Leigh Ann was just about to share a new project with us."

Leigh Ann reclaimed her perch on the sectional and then opened and closed her mouth twice before taking her work out of her folder. "You know I've written historical romance before, but this is something totally new for me—"

"No disclaimers," Monique reminded her.

Leigh Ann nodded, and began reading.

" 'From the moment their eyes met at last evening's ball, Adeline knew that Joseph, the darkly handsome and rakish young Romanian count, could never be an ordinary lover. But what could he possibly be doing here, standing in the dim light of the doorway of one of London's seedier pubs?'

" 'Startled, she caught her breath. She should never have been out so late. It was unseemly for a young woman of her station, so recently married, to go anywhere alone, especially at that late hour, but her mother had taken ill, the servants were out, her husband away on business, and someone had to go to the apothecary.'"

"The servants were out?" Teri interrupted. "What century did you say this was?"

"Save it," Monique warned, and Teri settled down.

" 'His gaze caught her own,'" Leigh Ann continued, throwing Teri an ugly look. " 'It stopped her cold. Something was not right. Her breast heaving with fear, she gathered her skirts, bunching them at her waist, terrified of the night, terrified of the lone man, terrified of herself. Yet, she could not tear herself away from that one stolen glance.'"

With all that terror, Jennifer thought, Leigh Ann's story was beginning to sound more like a horror story than a romance.

" 'Joseph kicked off from the wall and slowly, lyrically, flowed toward her. He lifted her hands, pulling them from the rich brocade of her skirts, and brought them first one and then the other to his lips.'"

" 'She swooned, even as her lips parted in a faint "no," her head falling against his muscled chest. He held her tightly. She relaxed against his strength, mesmerized, her eyes drifting shut, safe, secure, until she realized something was amiss. Her ear, pressed against the soft gauze of his shirt, heard nothing. The soft thump of a beating heart was not there!'"

Not a good sign.

" 'Adeline struggled back as Joseph's lips parted, his head rearing back in a demonic grin, his inch-long incisors glinting in the dim light. She screamed as he plunged his teeth into the milky white flesh of her—'"

"Whoa!" Teri interrupted. "Your hero is a vampire?"

Leigh Ann gave her a look that would have killed a normal person.

It only encouraged Teri. "Hello! Your hero doesn't have a heart!"

"Technically, no, but that doesn't mean he can't be a good person."

"Yes it does," Jennifer insisted. "She's married, and there's no way you can justify adultery and still have it be a romance, even if she's *mesmerized*. Besides, he just tore her throat out. How romantic is that?"

"Two teeny-weeny wounds. That's all. They won't even leave a scar."

"Kind of a 'love' nip, huh?" April added, back to her old self. "By the way, I think you should reconsider using the word *demonic*. Not very heroic. And those teeth! Unless they're retractable, they make this guy totally unattractive. I don't care what else comes with the package." She shifted uncomfortably.

"You all right?" Jennifer asked.

"Uh-huh," April managed, her teeth clenched. "Just give me a second."

Monique ignored April, obviously upset with Leigh Ann. Her face had taken on a purplish hue. "And your market research shows . . ." She raised a powerful eyebrow.

Leigh Ann licked her lips. "Vampires are all the rage, surely your know that. Ever since Anne Rice—"

"Oooh, Tom Cruise and Brad Pitt," April cut in, apparently all better again. "If anyone could make vampires sexy, even with that hair—"

Teri nodded. "Lose the hair, but a definite improvement over Bela Lugosi."

"Different era, different style. I'm sure Lugosi was quite chic for his time." Jennifer couldn't believe she was defending the sex appeal of a horror icon.

"No no no!" Leigh Ann insisted. "Joseph is just an extreme version of the alpha male. Some recent books—"

Monique shook her head. "The movie April cited is several years old, and so is the public's interest in vampires. Who knows how long that trend will run?" She cleared her throat. "Need I remind you? You're an *unpublished* author, Leigh Ann—"

Yeah. As if she—or any of them—might have forgotten.

Leigh Ann jutted out her chin. "I prefer the term *prepublished*."

"Fine. While you remain in your *pre*-published state,

let me caution you to play it safe. What we're seeing in the stores right now has been a good two years in the making. Add another year for you to write your book plus a year to get it through production, assuming it's bought as soon as you finish it, and you're already four years behind those recent books before you even start. Better stick with tried and true themes that are always around, at least for your first sale."

The business of writing could be *so* depressing. Jennifer had seen it get in the way of the art before. It could kill the joy of it, and if they weren't getting paid, why were they writing if not for the joy?

April made a loud "Sssssst" sound by sucking in air hard against her teeth. Her eyes squinted shut and she had a pained expression upon her face.

"You sure you're all right?" Jennifer asked.

"Uh-huh," April repeated in a tone higher than before. Then she relaxed, blinked, and looked almost normal. "Go ahead," she insisted.

Must have been a cramp.

Jennifer looked back at Leigh Ann, who had thrown herself into the plumpness of the sofa. She couldn't see Joseph as a hero—heartless, diabolical, cold—but some women, good women, did fall for men like that, and it wasn't her story to tell.

"Write whatever you want," Jennifer told her, fully aware she was bucking Monique's authority and that there would most likely be a price to pay. "If this is the story that speaks to you, then write it. But if you're doing it only because someone else has done it, you don't stand a prayer." It was the best advice she had to give, and the only advice that made any sense.

Teri jumped in. "But if you're writing romance, don't forget we gals have certain ideas about what makes our men appealing. The need for regular blood transfusions ain't one of them."

April rolled to one side and pushed herself up. She managed to get her feet firmly under herself and stood, swaying a little. "Don't mind me. You all go ahead. I'll be back in a minute." She tottered down the hall toward the bathroom.

"I hope she's all right," Jennifer said.

Teri nodded. "She's fine. Some kind of Braxton-Hicks something or other. When I talked to her earlier today, she told me she'd been having them all morning."

"Braxton-Hicks? Oh my . . ." Monique was on her feet.

"What?" Leigh Ann demanded.

"Braxton-Hicks are false labor pains," Monique explained. "You don't have Braxton-Hicks when you're past your due date."

Teri licked her lips, her eyes wide. "You don't mean . . ."

Jennifer caught up with Monique, who'd already made it to the powder room and had her ear pressed to the closed door. She shushed Jennifer, who suddenly seemed incapable of forming a whole word.

Leigh Ann and Teri were right behind them.

"Yo, April," Teri called out, wedging herself between Monique and Jennifer and pounding on the door. "You all right in there?"

Leigh Ann slapped at her, but Teri totally ignored her.

"April?" Jennifer called, finding her voice at last.

April's words were muffled through the wood. "I think I could use some help in here."

Chapter 32

What struck Jennifer most about the whole birthing process was how, like death, no matter how many people were around a woman, she had to do it alone.

"Can we see her?" Teri asked Jennifer again, like a little kid tugging on a grown-up's sleeve.

Teri had surprised them all by being the one who'd taken charge when they opened that bathroom door and realized if they didn't get an ambulance to Monique's right away, they were all about to become unlicensed midwives. Teri had made the 911 call, calmly giving directions, and then relayed what they were to do over the phone.

Jennifer secretly suspected that her calm was a desperate attempt to keep that phone in her hands, so she wouldn't be called upon to do anything else. Not that there was all that much to do, except smooth April's hair, run a wet washcloth over her forehead, hold her hand, and tell her everything would be fine.

Her water had broken, but the paramedics made it in less than five minutes. All that was left was to usher them in and then follow the ambulance to the hospital.

"Craig will let us know when it's time for us to go in," Jennifer assured Teri. "April needs a little time with him and Jonathan and the baby. As a family. Besides, her

173

mom and dad are in there, too. And her brothers and sister. We're second string."

"More like third or fourth," Teri declared.

"You can go home if you want," Jennifer told her. "I know April will understand."

"Go home? After we practically delivered that child ourselves? You've got to be kidding. The least she can do is name her after us: Teri Jennifer Leigh. Sounds good, don't ya think?"

"You left out Monique."

"So?"

Teri didn't even live with a pretense of fairness.

"Why don't you read something?" Jennifer suggested. "Or catch up to Leigh Ann and Monique at the snack machine. Who knows what they'll bring back." Or when, especially with Leigh Ann checking out the interns. "If Craig comes out for us, I'll give you a holler."

Teri nodded and took off down the hallway, leaving Jennifer alone for the first time all evening. She'd called to let Sam and the girls know that April's little girl had made her debut, so they wouldn't worry. She had no idea what time she'd get home. It was close to two in the morning, and she was exhausted. Again.

She opened the bag she always took to critique meetings and fished inside for something to occupy herself with. Her hand landed on the folder from the fertility clinic, the one Monique had gotten during their office visit. She'd looked through it, shoved it in the bag, and forgotten all about it.

Inside was a questionnaire like the one Monique had refused to fill out, along with some newsletters proclaiming the clinic's miraculous achievements, and a brochure that described the various procedures with gross little line drawings and, of course, a fee schedule. This was definitely not a poor man's game. Another sheet listed the success rates and how they were to be interpreted—read manipulated. And still another told about the physicians and their backgrounds.

She scanned down through Paul Collier's credentials. Pretty impressive. On paper. So were McEvoy's and Sullivan's. She found Donald's name near the bottom. He'd been the last to join the group.

Washington, D.C., jumped out at her as if it had been printed in boldface type. She sat up as though she'd been stung by a bee. That's where Donald had worked before coming to Macon. She never would have caught it if Sam hadn't given her that little geography lesson. Could he have been there fourteen years ago? Johnny had said something about a scandal concerning some of Donald's patients. Her hands trembled against the paper. Could the Turners have been those patients?

Teri thrust a cold can of ginger ale into her hand, and Leigh Ann dumped a package of chocolate doughnut gems into her lap.

"Jeez, Jen. What's wrong? Did something happen to April?" Teri demanded, plopping down next to her on one of the slick molded chairs.

"No. She's fine," Jennifer insisted, stuffing the folder back into her bag and trying to get her face out of crisis mode.

"Then what's up with you? The baby's born, and the mom's out of recovery. Most natural process in the world, I'm told. Not that I ever intend to find out. Did I miss something? For a minute there you looked really scary."

She'd found the link. Or had she? So what if Donald

had lived in the same general area as the Turners? It hardly explained how Diane got from that house in Bethesda to his brother's clinic. If, indeed, she actually was Cat Turner.

A lean, smiling Craig emerged from the hallway carrying a sleepy, towheaded Jonathan snuggled against his daddy's neck, his chubby little thumb slipping from his lips as his eyes gave in to sleep. He was undoubtedly the cutest ragamuffin of a two-year-old Jennifer had ever seen. Every time she was around him, he weakened her resolve. Writing didn't compare to the miracle that would someday be her Jaimie.

"The family's finally cleared out, and April wants to see you guys," Craig announced, beaming. He shifted his son to his other shoulder.

They all stood, and Jennifer reached out for Jonathan. Craig gratefully handed him to her. He'd probably been holding him all night.

The toddler briefly opened his eyes and then settled into Jennifer's arms as though he belonged there. Then Jennifer, Teri, Leigh Ann, and Monique followed Craig back to April's room.

They found her propped up on pillows, both more exhausted and more radiant than Jennifer had ever seen her. She looked like she'd been hosed down and left to dry, but her face . . . it glowed. In the crook of her arm was a bundle that wiggled and squirmed. Framed by a pink blanket was a tiny, wrinkled face with a perfectly formed doll-like nose. Her impossibly small hands stretched out, fingers splayed and then snuggled back. Then she hiccuped a brief squeal of displeasure and yawned. Suddenly two dark eyes opened, assessing the crew and her strange new world.

April grinned. "Got somebody for you all to meet."

Leigh Ann touched the blanket. "April, she's precious. Would you look at all that dark hair, and in a family of blondes, too. You takin' after your Aunt Leigh, sweetie?"

"You can't tell what color my hair's going to be yet," Monique said in a cooing kind of baby-talk voice, bending over the bed. "My little eyes could even turn brown for all we know, couldn't they?" She offered her pinky to the baby, who grabbed onto it. "Yes, they could." She grinned and shook the tiny fist attached over her fingernail.

Maybe Monique wasn't quite the ogre Jennifer had her pegged.

Teri dug at the bottom of the blanket and uncovered a foot. "How does something that puny grow so big?" she asked.

"You want a closer look, Jen?" April asked.

"That's all right. I can see from here," she said from the foot of the bed, cradling Jonathan's head against her shoulder. "I've kind of got my hands full right now. She sure is gorgeous."

"Isn't she though," April agreed, beaming. "You know, she's not even two hours old, and I already love her more than my own life."

That's how nature had planned it. That bond, so strong, so surprising to a first-time mother. Had Beverly Hoffman experienced it when her son was born? Was that why she had agreed to help Diane? Had she resented Paul Collier for taking her child even if she'd agreed to it in advance? Even if he'd fulfilled his promise to put her through school and give her a job?

Handing that baby over must have been heart-wrenching. Was that why Beverly wanted to counsel surrogates, to make sure they knew? Did she want to make sure Paul never did to anyone else what he had done to her?

Chapter 33

"I don't see how this could happen," Jennifer insisted, peering over the high back of her airplane seat. "I'm sure when I made the reservations, our seats were all together."

Sam was so far back she could barely see his head past the rows and rows of people.

"Must be some computer glitch, doll," Johnny told her. "No big deal. Relax. Enjoy." He sat with his hat cocked down over his eyes, a self-satisfied smirk on his face.

A little too self-satisfied. Jennifer took note of the seat next to hers, the one against the window, the one with nobody in it.

She settled back down and slid her carry-on bag out from in front of her feet toward the window. She barely had room to stretch out her legs, and the tightness of the seats put her closer to Johnny than she'd ever hoped to be. He'd already appropriated their shared armrest. It was going to be a long flight. She could tell.

The seat belt sign went on, and she buckled up.

The pilot's voice came on over the intercom, smooth and competent. "I want to welcome you aboard our flight from Atlanta to Reagan National Airport in Arlington, Virginia. The weather is clear with temperatures close to a high of fifty degrees today. We'll be in the air approximately fifty-nine minutes. I hope you enjoy your flight, and thanks for choosing us as your air carrier."

The engines started their whine and the plane moved forward, giving Jennifer that little thrill in the pit of her stomach she never quite got used to. She knew she was safer in an airplane than in a car, yet . . .

Johnny leaned in. "You okay? You're looking a little green."

"Fine. Great." At least she would be once they got off the ground. "Where'd you go after you threw me out of your condo the other morning?"

He tilted his hat back, and she could see his eyes. He needed to lay off of whatever it was he drank for his supper, let the blood in his eyes go back to wherever it belonged.

"Threw you out? I must have been drunker than I thought."

He kind of groaned, and she noticed his hands starting to shake. He searched in his coat pocket and came up with something he popped in his mouth. Nicotine gum. It had to be. Thank goodness. She'd been worried about him trying to light up and getting them all thrown off the plane.

"As I see it, we've got two principals." He gave the gum a chew and then tucked it between his cheek and his gum, making a small bulge. "Paul and Donald Collier, especially with Donald's involvement with the D.C. clinic. So I thought I'd do a little more snooping, see what I could find out about them. You know, what they're into, that sort of thing."

"Yeah, and . . . ?"

"And not much. The clinic keeps them hoppin'. Lots of clients. Lots of cash coming in. Paul likes the limelight. He keeps a presence in a number of civic organizations, gives them money more than time. Makes for good PR."

"He doesn't go to church."

Johnny nodded. "No church. He hunts. Deer, mostly. But he'll settle for squirrel, pheasant, most anything in season."

Jennifer winced. "Into killing things, huh?"

"It's legal."

"And Donald?"

"He's more the fisherman type. Freshwater. Lake mostly. Got a cabin on Lake Tobesofkee."

"A cabin? That's pretty built up out there. Lots of really nice homes."

"Yeah. Well, seems he bought several acres when he first came out here years ago in an area away from all that development. The woods run back a good distance. Not all of it is lakefront property. Likes it feral."

Now there was a word she hadn't expected Johnny to know.

"Any run-ins with the law?" she asked. It'd be nice if it were that simple. Charged with a count or two of baby selling. Or baby stealing.

"Not even a civil suit."

"You've got to be kidding."

"Nope."

"Considering what they do, that's hard to believe."

"Unless they're in the habit of paying off anyone who's not satisfied," Johnny said.

His hand brushed hers, and she drew back. Sharing an armrest was awkward. She hoped it'd been an accident.

"You're all business, aren't you, Marsh?" He said it like it was a statement.

Absolutely. As business as she could get.

"You ought to learn how to play a little, ease up some." He shifted in his seat and stared at her, an intense, get-my-drift kind of stare.

"You know the food on these flights is great," she said,

pulling her snack bag out of the seat-back pocket in front of her. "Just look what all we've got. Bagels"—it looked like it had been sat on, but that was because she'd crammed it into the pocket with no intention of eating it—"cream cheese, orange juice, banana. Yummy." She grabbed his bag and shoved it into his hands.

"Eat your bagel," Jennifer insisted. Translation: put something in your mouth so you can't talk.

The flight attendant started her demonstration of the oxygen masks and the flotation devices. Fifty-nine minutes, huh? Only fifty-seven left. It was going to be a really long flight.

"You know what I like most about you, Marsh?" Johnny asked, stuffing his unopened snack bag into the pocket.

She didn't know, and she really, really didn't want to.

"You're smart," he said, and settled back into his seat. Maybe it wouldn't be such a long flight after all.

Fortunately, most things have an end, and so did that flight. Once on the ground, Jennifer insisted they split up. She'd had about all she could tolerate of her so-called partner for the time being. Johnny went off to check out the clinic where Donald Collier had once been an associate, and Jennifer and Sam to meet with Lou Myers, Montgomery County police.

"How'd you get Myers to agree to see us so soon?" Sam asked, stirring his strawberry milkshake with a straw in the slick gray-and-pink booth at the Silver Diner on Rockville Pike.

"Simple. I told him I had the little girl that disappeared from the Turners' home the night of their deaths."

"Jennifer, you know you can't—"

She nudged him under the table with her foot. "Dark

blue suit coming in at twelve o'clock. He's scanning the place. I think he's our man."

She waved at him, a big, barrel-chested man, and he came over.

"Ms. Marsh?"

She nodded. "Detective Myers?"

Sam moved over and Myers slipped in beside him. His hair was gray and thin with peach fuzz on top, most likely the result of Rogaine. He adjusted his tie as though his collar were a little too tight and then ordered a cup of coffee from the waitress, who had followed him over.

"So, you know where Cynthia Turner is?"

"I think so," Jennifer told him.

He nodded. "The disappearance of that child always bothered me. It didn't add up."

"How so?" Sam asked.

Myers looked him up and down.

"Sam Culpepper. I spoke with you by phone."

"Right." They shook hands. "Why was she missing? If the father shot the mother, then killed himself, why wasn't the child still in the house? The door was locked. It wasn't as if a kid that size would let herself out and then lock the place back up."

"A third party," Sam offered.

He nodded. "Had to be."

"You think somebody else killed them?" Jennifer asked.

"Don't know. Turner fired the gun, no doubt about it. He had powder residue all over his right hand. We didn't find any stray bullets, and only two were missing from the clip. And it appears he shot himself. The bullet went in at close range. But who shoots himself in the chest to commit suicide?"

"Any evidence of a struggle?" Sam asked.

"Sure. But that's to be expected. This wasn't no suicide pact. Mrs. Turner didn't go down willingly."

Jennifer sucked hard on the straw of her chocolate shake. "So who was the other person?"

He shook his head. "We questioned friends, neighbors, coworkers. Never came up with anything that led anywhere. How'd you find the girl?"

"She sort of found us," Jennifer said.

Myers signaled the waitress to refill his coffee. "So what makes you think it's her?"

"She was adopted at age three under less than normal circumstances," Sam explained, "and she told her adopted mother that her name was Cat."

"Yeah, and . . . ?"

"And there's a tag." Jennifer pulled it out of her pocket and showed it to Myers. "We need to know if that phone number belonged to the Turners fourteen years ago."

Myers rubbed his fingers over the metal, studying the engraving.

"That's easy enough to do." He pulled a cell phone out of his pocket and dialed. "Hey, Pete," he said into the phone. "Do me a favor and get the file on the Turner case. It's on my desk . . . Yeah. The fourteen-year-old murder/suicide that happened in Bethesda . . . No, man. Now. It won't take you five minutes. Just check out the home phone number of the victims. Then call me back." He stuffed the phone back into his jacket.

"If we get a match, I want an interview," he told them. "If the child was there that night—and as best we can tell she must have been—she might have seen what happened."

Jennifer could feel her cheeks grow red. "She was only three. She doesn't remember anything." She really hoped that was true.

He looked at her as though he wasn't so sure he believed her. "Children remember more than we think they do. Something that traumatic—"

"We haven't told her how her birth parents may have died. We want to know for sure before we hit her with something like that," Sam said. "But short of a DNA test—"

"We have her fingerprints," Myers interrupted. "They were all over the house, along with half a dozen other three-year-olds. And the parents had them done at one of those safety programs at the mall. Left them in a home file. If you can get me this girl's prints, we'll know. Could be off a glass, almost anything smooth she's handled."

"Okay," Jennifer agreed. "I'll send them to you."

The waitress refilled his coffee. Myers only had time to drink about half a cup before the phone in his pocket rang. Jennifer was into the last third of her shake. Sam had long since finished his.

"Yeah," Myers said into the mouthpiece. He fingered the disk as he listened. "Okay. Thanks." He hung up and looked straight at Jennifer. "We've got a match."

Myers' words took her breath away. She knew she was right. She had to be right. What other explanation could there have been? But having it confirmed . . .

"You said something to Sam over the phone about grandparents," she managed. "Are they still living?"

"One. The woman's mother. Last I heard, she was still around, but you've got to remember we've had no movement on this case for years."

"Would it be all right . . . I mean, I'd like to speak with her, if you think . . ." She was groping.

Sam frowned at her, probably a little more concerned than he should be about her state of mind.

Myers studied her. "I could take you over there, but you've got to be careful what you say. You can't show up on somebody's doorstep and start opening up old wounds without a bandage to hand them."

She looked at him funny.

"We get what we can, but we tell her nothing. No false hopes," Myers insisted.

She nodded. The last thing she wanted was to cause more pain to what was left of Diane's family.

Chapter 34

"Detective Myers," Mrs. Owens said, opening the door to the modest town house in Gaithersburg and drying her hands on a dish towel. She looked flustered and then wary. "You'll have to excuse me. I was just finishing up my lunch dishes. Won't you come in?"

There was a bit of the South in her voice. Not Georgian, Jennifer decided, maybe Virginian, most likely coastal.

Mrs. Owens ushered them into a small sitting room brightened by windows that ran across the front of the house. She was petite, painfully thin, with a gray cardigan over a simple tailored dress. She showed them to a floral print sofa and then sat, folding the towel across the arm of her upholstered chair.

She asked no questions, and Jennifer could guess she'd had more answers from Myers than she'd ever wanted.

"Miss Marsh wanted to speak with you," Myers told her, sitting back.

Jennifer leaned forward, daring to touch her hand. "I'm sorry about your loss," she said. Stupid, inadequate words, but she meant them.

The woman drew back and peered at her as though she didn't care a fig about what Jennifer was sorry about. Her armor was well in place.

"I . . . I wonder if you'd mind telling me about your daughter and your son-in-law."

"You're not starting up another investigation, are you?" Mrs. Owens turned to Myers. "Has something happened? You said it was cut and dried . . . Oh my . . . Cynthia. You've found Cynthia's body."

The woman went chalk-white.

Jennifer vigorously shook her head. "Nothing like that." Myers had warned her. He shook his head ever so slightly at her. "You called your granddaughter Cynthia?"

"Of course. That was her name."

"Did she happen to have a stuffed pink cat?"

That one hit home. "We never found it. The police asked me to go through her clothes to see if I could tell what she'd been wearing that night. Do you know how impossible that is? It's like looking at one of those pictures and trying to figure out what's different, only I didn't have anything to compare it with. The child had enough clothes to dress a village. But the cat . . . she always had hold of that shabby old toy. I missed it right away."

"Could it have had a tag, maybe around its neck?" Jennifer asked.

"It said, 'Cat's cat.' Her father called her Cat. My God. You found it." The woman covered her mouth. The control she had so firmly in place disappeared. She looked very old and terribly vulnerable.

"Mrs. Owens, we don't know what we've found," Myers explained.

"Oh no, you don't," Mrs. Owens insisted with the strength of the righteous. "You *will not* come into this house and mention my precious granddaughter and think you can walk back out without telling me a word. That child was Colette's whole world. She and Robert had been trying to conceive for years before she finally became pregnant—"

"How had they been trying?" Sam asked quietly.

Jennifer was sure of the answer before she heard it.

"They went to a fertility clinic, two actually. The first one couldn't help them."

"Was one in Washington, D.C.?" Sam asked.

"The second. How did you know?" Mrs. Owens studied Sam.

Sam shrugged. "Just a guess."

"Did your daughter know a Dr. Donald Collier?" Jennifer added.

"Collier?" Mrs. Owens repeated.

"He specializes in fertility procedures," Sam explained.

She seemed to be mulling the name over in her mind, but then she shook her head. "She could have. I don't remember her ever mentioning that name."

"Obviously, someone was able to help. Your daughter did get pregnant," Jennifer said.

"It wasn't her problem; it was her husband's. I'm not sure what they did, but Cynthia was born less than two years after they found the second clinic. We were all thrilled." Mrs. Owens took up the dish towel, plucked at it, then folded and unfolded it on her lap.

Myers nodded toward the door.

"We've got to be going," Jennifer said, standing up.

Mrs. Owens grabbed her hand. "You still haven't told me. Is my granddaughter alive or dead?"

What should she say? Diane was quite alive, and, with every fiber of her being, Jennifer felt sure she was Cynthia. But it wasn't her call. False hope could be a kind of death of its own. She looked to Myers.

"We should know soon," Myers told her.

"After fourteen years . . ." she said. "That poor baby. I don't even know if her leg healed."

"Was she injured?" Jennifer asked, sitting back down on the edge of the sofa.

"The week they . . . the week this all happened, Cynthia was playing on the jungle gym in the backyard. She fell, suffering a compound fracture to her lower leg. Lost a lot of blood. Scared us all half to death. She'd have a scar somewhere about mid-calf. I think it was her right leg. It's funny. That's what I tend to wonder about. Not if she's alive, but if her leg healed all right."

We all have our defense mechanisms.

At the door, she turned and thanked Mrs. Owens.

"I don't know what for," the woman said. "I don't really mind talking about it. It's not like I don't think about it most every day, one way or another. If I could only understand. . . ."

"Understand what?" Jennifer asked.

"Why he killed her. Why he killed my daughter."

Chapter 35

Jennifer insisted that Myers take them past what had been the Turners' house. She didn't know why she had to see it, only that she did. As if viewing where the horror had occurred would somehow make her understand.

It was a brick colonial in an older Bethesda neighborhood full of stately homes and lots of trees beginning to shed their leaves. A wreath of dried, burnt-orange flowers and leaves in yellows and browns hung on the front door. A child's bike and some push toys rested on the front stoop.

It all seemed so sad. So totally unnecessary. Once she'd seen it, she couldn't get away fast enough.

Their flight left at 5:45 P.M. They'd barely had time to meet up with Johnny before boarding. They carried along their "snack" supper as they made their way through the boarding tunnels to an all-too-familiar row of claustrophobia-inducing seats. She didn't know how commuters did this on a regular basis. Twice in one day was way too much for her.

This time, when the doors closed and before the plane lifted off, Sam appeared in the aisle next to Johnny. He didn't say a word, just grumbled and pushed past them, settling into the seat next to the window.

Leaving Jennifer a human buffer zone. With no arm-rest of her own.

She waited until the plane lifted off and Johnny had his required dose of nicotine before turning to him. "So give. What'd you find out at the clinic?"

"You could work on your interviewing technique, doll. Kind of brusque," he told her, leaning out into the aisle to check out a dark-haired attendant who was distributing pillows.

"You don't want me mad," she warned him, pushing his elbow off her armrest. She'd put up with him on the trip down; she wasn't up for an encore.

Sam was watching, an amused look on his face.

"Hey, all right," he said, shifting in his seat and turning toward her. "Took me some sweet talk to get the information."

Yeah, right. She'd believe a fifty dollar bill.

"Donald Collier was the Turners' physician, just as you suspected. Mr. Turner had a . . . you know . . . a low count, as in practically nonexistent."

Hah! She didn't know Johnny knew how to blush.

"Anyhow," he went on, "they did whatever it is they do in those situations, and Mrs. Turner came up pregnant. She transferred to the care of an obstetrician, and baby Turner appeared nine months later."

"And that was it?"

"Yeah. Except for follow-up visits by Mrs. Turner."

Jennifer nodded. There had to be something else, some other link. As far as she was concerned, sending Diane's fingerprints to Myers was simply a formality. She had no doubt that Diane was Cat. Now if she only had a clue how Cat had become Diane . . .

"When did Donald leave the practice?"

Johnny grinned at her as though he'd been waiting for that question. "Thirteen years ago. You can add six months to that if you want to get technical. The Turners had been his patients, and their deaths didn't reflect well."

"But that was three years before."

"Yeah, but Mrs. Turner was still under his care. And you don't go messin' with something as volatile as baby makin' if you've got some unstable individual involved. He should have screened them out. Collier's colleagues weren't so happy about the publicity, so—"

"So he abandoned ship and threw in with brother Paul," she finished. That was one way to look at it, she supposed.

Sam nudged her from the other side. He'd been listening and, fortunately, not commenting. "What are you going to tell her?"

Why was it always left for women to deal with situations like this? As if she could cushion the blow better than a man. She glanced at Sam and then Johnny. Maybe there was a reason they left these things to women.

She ran her tongue over her lips. They felt dry. Her whole mouth felt dry. "If I tell her—"

"When," Sam said.

He was right. She wasn't getting out of this one, whether it was now or later. "When I tell her, she might remember something."

"Don't count on it."

"I'm not. I'm hoping she won't." She wished she could somehow back up, get some perspective. She was identifying far too closely with Diane. Like Mrs. Owens, she seemed stuck on the details.

But they'd made some major progress. Now they knew the who, at least as far as Diane was concerned. And part of the what. They still had to figure out the how and the why.

She let her eyes drift shut. Mrs. Owens had given her another question to add to her list: Why had Turner killed his wife?

Think, Jennifer, she told herself. She'd glided right over that question before, dismissing it as totally irrelevant. She'd been so intent on finding out *who* Diane was, she missed the bigger issue. Leigh Ann had tried to tell her, but she wouldn't listen. Maybe it wasn't why she was *adopted*; maybe it was why *she* was adopted. Because her father had killed her mother and then committed suicide. Or had he? Somebody else had a stake in what happened to Diane. But why?

She sat up, her eyes wide open. It was all starting to make sense. Why Diane had disappeared from Bethesda, why she'd been given to the Robbinses, why money mysteriously appeared in their bank account every August 14, why Diane was on full scholarship when kids with close to perfect grades were having trouble getting grants.

She needed to make a phone call to Myers as soon as they landed. He could find out the information she needed to confirm her suspicions.

There was never a black market baby operation. Diane had not been sold. She was carefully placed and carefully watched over. No wonder no one had bothered them since the break-in at her apartment. There'd been no need.

But the noose was tightening. The trip to Maryland had shown their hand when they didn't even know they were holding one.

And she had made one major mistake. She should never have let Diane out of her sight, not now, not after they knew she was Cat.

While Diane obviously had a benefactor, it was just as

obvious that someone else would stop at nothing to keep the past buried. Beverly Hoffman's murder proved that.

She struggled against the seat belt. "Can't this plane go any faster?" she complained.

Chapter 36

"Stop here!" Jennifer insisted to Sam, tumbling out of his Honda in front of the stairs to Unit 207 of the Residence Inn on Macon's north side. Johnny was out of the backseat before she hardly had her door open. Her heart raced as she ran up the steps right behind him. His wound was still fresh enough to give him trouble. He was breathing hard when they got to the top.

The sun had long since gone down, but the place was well-lit. Light streamed from the door, which was standing open. When Jennifer walked in, Anne Marie, her face streaked with tears, fell into her arms.

"They're gone," she sobbed.

"When?" Jennifer asked, trying to take in what had happened.

"I don't know. Hours ago. I went out to bring something back for supper. Valerie insisted she had to have some pork barbecue. I had to go all the way across town, and then I had to wait. When I got back, they weren't here."

Sam burst through the doorway. "What's going on?"

"The girls have disappeared. Valerie engineered the whole thing, I'm sure," Jennifer told him.

"Valerie?" Anne Marie said. "But she's Diane's roommate."

"She's been passing information, I'm sure of it."

"She couldn't have. She's a college student," Anne Marie insisted.

"That, too. Most likely she's getting a little money every month for her services. I doubt she has any idea what she's done."

"But who—"

"I'm not sure. Maybe from the same person behind the Elliot Woodrow scholarship. You had to suspect something," Jennifer told Anne Marie, helping her to sit down in a side chair. "Did you really think Diane's grades were good enough to merit that kind of grant? Or were you simply used to money and gifts showing up unexpectedly where Diane was concerned?"

"It seemed innocuous enough, and if someone wanted to help her out—"

"How long have you known Diane is Donald Collier's daughter?" Jennifer asked.

Sam grabbed her arm. "Did I miss something?"

Anne Marie shook her head and turned her back. "I swear I don't know what you're talking about." She was like a little kid covering her ears. She didn't want to hear it. She'd had her head stuck in the sand so long, she'd long since lost any desire to know. If she'd ever had it.

Johnny put a warning hand on Jennifer's other arm. "She doesn't know, doll. Didn't any of them know about the Bethesda connection till you uncovered it."

"Listen to me," Jennifer insisted, tugging at Anne Marie's sleeve.

Reluctantly, Anne Marie turned back around.

"Your daughter may be in danger. It's time to put all our resources together. You can't hide from this any longer.

"We'll need to get Myers to check out the blood types," she told Sam and Johnny, "but I'm sure now of what happened. Donald and Colette either fell in love, or she simply saw a way to get what she wanted: a child. And she could do it without her husband ever suspecting. Or so she thought.

"Who knows what Donald's motives were?" Jennifer continued. "Maybe he simply found Colette attractive. In any case, Colette realized her husband was never going to be a father, at least not with the technology available at that time. Mrs. Owens said they'd been to another clinic that couldn't help them before going to the one in D.C."

"But why the murder/suicide?" Sam asked.

"That was the key. Why did Turner kill his wife? Mrs. Owens gave us the answer when she said Diane had been injured."

"Her leg," Anne Marie said. "She had a cast on her leg when we got her."

"Yes. She said she'd lost a lot of blood. The injury happened the same week as the murder. She was only three years old. The doctors had to be concerned she might need a blood transfusion, whether they actually did one or not."

"Which means they'd type her blood," Sam threw in.

"And maybe the blood of her parents, one of whom would likely be a match. Even if they didn't, most adults know their blood types," Jennifer said.

"But—" Sam started.

"The types didn't match," Jennifer said, "and Robert—"

"Realized he wasn't Diane's father."

"Mrs. Turner panicked—"

"And called Donald Collier—"

"Who must have gone to the house and witnessed the confrontation or at least part of the horror that followed," Jennifer concluded.

"Are you saying," Anne Marie said, trying to make

sense out of their Ping-Pong conversation, "that Donald Collier took Diane from that house?"

"He couldn't just leave her there, not with her parents lying dead in the house. She *was* his child," Jennifer said. "He must have been horrified by the thought of her seeing them like that."

"Collier figures if he leaves without her," Johnny said, "the kid goes into the child welfare system. Then the only way he can lay claim to her—if that's what he wants to do—is by confessing that he's the father. Not so good for business."

"That, and maybe he didn't want anybody asking her any questions about what happened that night," Sam added.

"But how did Diane get to Macon?" Anne Marie asked.

"My guess would be brother Paul," Jennifer suggested. "Donald must have called him, asking for help. Donald couldn't keep the child with him. He had a wife at home who would be asking more questions than he would care to answer. He probably hadn't even considered the implications when he took Diane. He just wanted her out of there."

"So you figure either Paul came up and got Diane or Donald flew down with her," Johnny said.

"Right. Paul knew how much you and your husband wanted a child," Jennifer told Anne Marie, "and that you couldn't afford to continue fertility treatments. There was nothing to link Donald with the Turners except professionally, so who would suspect? His rendezvous with Colette most likely took place in his office. All she had to do was make an appointment. And no one would be looking for Diane in another state."

"But why do you think Valerie had something to do with all this?" Anne Marie asked.

"When I went to Lanier to get the girls their books," Jennifer said, "I saw the room. Only half of it had been searched—Diane's half. Who would know which was which? The furniture all looks the same. No one saw anyone suspicious in the dorm that night, and it was Diane who reported the incident to her residence director, *after* coming home and finding Valerie in the room. I suspect Valerie's plan was to search for the envelope from Hoffman and then put everything back like it was. It wasn't to anybody's advantage to scare Diane off campus."

"Only Valerie got herself caught," Johnny added, "when Diane came home earlier than expected from your apartment."

Jennifer nodded. "And then when Diane came to us, Valerie had no choice but to come along."

"That way she was privy to everything you said and did," Johnny added.

"Diane told me that while you and I were out," Jennifer said, turning to Sam, "Valerie went through all your closets and drawers on the pretext of looking for a Ouija board. I think she was making sure we didn't have whatever Beverly had planned to give Johnny that night in the alley. And then there was that time she left your place supposedly to get doughnuts. She probably went out to make a phone call, to check in.

"But most compelling of all, she had to be the leak about Hoffman meeting Johnny in the alley that night. Only four of us knew: Johnny, Hoffman, me, and Diane. Neither Johnny nor I told anyone. Hoffman would have been crazy to mention it to anyone. But Diane most surely told Valerie. She'd been with her when she found the clinic. She knew everything that was going on every step of the way, and that's why there was never another threat at Sam's apartment. There was no need."

"But where is Diane? Where would they take her and why?" Anne Marie asked.

"That all depends on who *they* are, on who hired Valerie. If it's Donald, I can't imagine him actually hurting Diane. In his own way, he's been more involved with her life than a lot of fathers. If it's Paul . . . Somebody paid to stop Beverly."

"All of this over saving a child through an illegal adoption?" Anne Marie blanched and her hands shook. It was lucky she was sitting down.

Jennifer shook her head. "There's something more, something we're missing." She started to pace. "Has to be to justify the murder and this kind of cover-up."

"Something that may come back to Diane if she learns enough of the story," Sam said.

Jennifer nodded, coming back to them. "She recognized Beverly Hoffman's eyes. Strange even to a three-year-old. If she witnessed the murder . . . Has she ever seen Donald or Paul, that you know of, since she was three, I mean?"

"No. Never," Anne Marie assured her.

"It might bring it all back—seeing them," Sam said.

"And that's when it could get really dangerous," Jennifer said.

"Then we've got to find them," Anne Marie declared. "Now."

But how?

Chapter 37

"Johnny." Jennifer grabbed hold of his jacket sleeve and shook it. "You've investigated Paul and Donald. Where would they have taken her? Someplace where there wouldn't be any people around."

He shook his head. "Not likely they did it together, but let's say it was Donald. He has a fishing cabin up on the lake, fairly isolated, likes to go up there for weekends. Could be the place."

"And Paul?" Sam asked.

"Paul hunts deer. He's got himself a trailer over in Jones County. I can get us to either one, but . . ."

He didn't finish the sentence, and Jennifer was grateful. They didn't have time to pick the wrong one. Diane's life might depend on it.

"Okay, we'll split up," Sam said.

Johnny nodded and turned. The two of them formed a huddle over by the breakfast bar. "You check out Donald's fishing cabin."

"Fine. I'm fairly familiar with the lake, so if you can give me some—"

"Oh no you don't. I'm going, too," Jennifer insisted, pulling them apart.

"If you think you're leaving me . . ." Anne Marie was immediately on her feet.

"All right, all right," Johnny said. "We don't have

time to argue." He looked at Sam. "We'll need to go by my place, to get some, you know, equipment."

Guns. Johnny had had to leave his guns at home because of the airplane flight. What did he think was going to happen? Did he think they were headed for a shoot-out?

Her everyday reality suffered a final death blow, leaving Jennifer caught in the strange and terrible world she'd stepped into that night in the alley, a world where real people could get hurt, people she knew and cared about.

"Shouldn't we be calling the police?" she asked, not at all happy.

"Sure. And then we can spend forty-five minutes to an hour explaining everything and trying to convince them we're not crazy while who knows what happens to Diane," Johnny said.

"I say screw 'em," Anne Marie threw in. "I hope you have enough equipment for me."

The world had gone mad. She'd promised Jaimie she wouldn't be in another shoot-out. She had promised, hadn't she?

"Okay, get me some paper," Johnny demanded, sitting on one of the stools at the bar.

Anne Marie found some motel stationery, and they all huddled around Johnny.

"I'm going to draw you a map as best I can remember. Keep in mind you're looking for something primitive. No running water, no electricity. Not much more than a place to store gear and get out of the weather if a storm comes up. It's hidden in the trees, but the road goes right down to it. Finding it will be the trick, especially in the dark. There aren't any lights out that way."

"You been there?" Sam asked.

"No. But I know what road it goes off of, and I know what the land's like out there."

Johnny put a compass in the upper right-hand corner and drew in some lines that he named as roads. "Now once you get here," he said, pointing with the pencil tip, "you're sure to lose the pavement. You can expect the road to turn rough. I think you'll be all right in your Honda, but—"

They heard steps on the stairs outside, and they all turned.

"I am *so* sorry," Valerie wailed as she came through the door. "I had no idea."

Jennifer grabbed her, afraid she might bolt when she saw what was going on, and pulled her over to the love seat in the other half of the suite.

"I didn't know," she babbled.

"Where's Diane?" Jennifer demanded, blocking Anne Marie with her body. The woman looked like she could tear Valerie limb from limb.

"I don't know. He gave me money. It's hard. School's so expensive."

"Who gave you money?"

"Paul Collier. He checked in every couple weeks or so, but I never had anything to tell him."

"But you told him about finding the clinic and about Diane fainting."

"Yeah. Of course. That's when he started calling me all the time, wanting to know what was going on. Diane even thought he was my boyfriend 'cause he wouldn't talk to her if she answered, just demanded to speak to me."

"A woman got killed," Johnny pointed out to her. He didn't add that he could have died as well.

"Paul said it was a drug theft. You mean . . ." Her eyes grew huge.

They looked at one another. It had been a long time since any of them were seventeen.

"So why'd you send Anne Marie out for barbecue?"

"He didn't know where we were, and he'd told me after we went to Sam's to let him know immediately if we changed locations. But I forgot the clinic was closed on Wednesday afternoons, so I got one of those answering machines, the nonemergency line. I said who I was and that I was calling for Paul Collier from the Residence Inn because you'd gone to Maryland. And to call me as soon as possible."

"So Paul's the one," Sam said.

"No," Valerie squealed. "It wasn't Paul. It was his brother Donald. He showed up here and gave Diane some song and dance about knowing who her real parents are. He said he would tell her everything, but she had to come with him for a little while. He had something important he had to do, but he wanted her to hear the story from him first. He seemed to know all of you. He dropped your names like you were old friends. Do you know him?"

"If Donald's got her, we don't have to worry so much, then, do we?" Anne Marie asked, trying to calm herself by taking long, deep breaths.

"Probably not," Sam agreed.

"Where'd he take her?" Johnny demanded.

"He scared me," Valerie said. "I thought he had a gun. He made me get in the car with them, and then he let me out on some two-lane road out in the country."

"On your way, did you go out past Wesleyan?" Sam asked.

"Yeah, I think so."

"West of the city, toward the lake," Johnny said.

"I don't know where I was," Valerie went on. "I walked until I found a house. The people were nice enough to let me make two phone calls. I called for a cab to bring me back here, and then I called Paul's home and told him what had happened."

"Oh, God," Anne Marie said, sinking into a nearby chair.

"Don't panic yet," Jennifer said. "At least we know where they are."

"And so does Paul," Sam added.

Chapter 38

Johnny was right. It was hard to see in the dark. Once they'd turned onto the dirt road, Sam cut all but his parking lights. The moon offered little help, only a sliver visible in the night sky.

The little Honda, especially with its load—Valerie and Anne Marie had insisted on coming—dragged over some of the rougher spots. Jennifer, wedged uncomfortably between the two women, had precious little room, but neither did she have a choice. She was afraid of what Anne Marie might do to Valerie. At least Johnny had refused her a gun when they'd stopped by the office, insisting he was "fresh out." He'd slipped one in Jennifer's pocket, the little pearl-handled number, and put his finger to his lips. It sagged against her thigh like the weight of the world. She knew she'd never be able to use it no matter what happened.

As they'd driven over, Sam made a phone call to the police, reporting a suspected kidnapping. Depending on the call's priority, they might even see a squad car before long. If they were lucky.

They were making no time at all. The road was totally unpredictable through the trees, and the parking lights might as well have been off. It had to be a difficult trip during the daytime. In the night and with almost no light, Sam found it necessary to drop to a snail's pace.

"But why?" Anne Marie said. Again.

Jennifer wished she'd just shut up. She was trying hard to focus on what they'd have to do once they got to the cabin, but Anne Marie's persistent question wouldn't let her. She thought she'd come up with the answer, but she hoped she was wrong.

She leaned forward toward the front seat, between Sam and Johnny. "If Donald was there the night the Turners died, it doesn't make sense. You don't kill someone and then commit suicide in front of a third party."

"What are you suggesting?" Sam asked, dodging a large rock and jolting Jennifer forward even more.

She braced herself between the seats. "What if the Turners had come back from the hospital, and Colette realized Robert knew their secret, that Diane wasn't his daughter? What if she called Donald?"

"Maybe from the hospital," Sam suggested.

"Whichever. But say Robert confronts her when they get home. He's furious, furious that Colette was unfaithful to him. He demands to know who Diane's father is. She tells him, which only adds to his anger. This is the man he trusted, the one he paid handsomely—as he now sees it—to sleep with his wife. He threatens her with a gun."

"About the time Donald makes his appearance," Johnny adds.

"Then or a little after. One way or the other, Donald discovers Robert has shot Colette." Her whole body tingled as all the clues finally fell into place. "Robert turns the gun on Donald, or, horrified at what he's done, turns the gun on himself. A struggle ensues. Robert is shot dead. In the chest, at close range. Whether Donald was protecting himself or trying to stop Robert from committing suicide, Donald has, in effect, killed Robert."

"So what we have now," Sam concluded, "is not a man simply rescuing his daughter from a crime scene, but a man who is responsible for another man's death."

"Now you're telling me my daughter's been abducted by a murderer?" Diane might not be Anne Marie's blood daughter, but she was every bit as ready to protect and defend that girl as any mother anywhere could be. Jennifer hoped Diane had even the slightest inkling of how much she was loved.

The next turn brought them almost smack into the rear bumper of a Rover or Jeep or some such vehicle pulled to the side of the narrow road. Sam threw on the brakes and they all flew forward and then fell back. Apparently, they had arrived.

In the dim light it looked like yet another four-wheel-drive vehicle was parked farther up in front, but Jennifer couldn't tell the make in the dark.

Even before Sam cut the motor, Jennifer heard the door latch unlock on Anne Marie's side. She turned and grabbed onto the woman for all she was worth, using all of her 120 pounds as dead weight to keep Anne Marie from escaping.

"You can't just run up to that cabin, assuming we're even in the right place. You want to get all of us killed?" Jennifer whispered loudly. She grabbed onto Valerie, too, for good measure.

"What?" Valerie asked, shrugging out of her grip.

"Just making sure. So, Johnny, what's the plan?" Jennifer asked, hopeful that he'd come up with something. After all, he'd had the whole car ride to do nothing but think.

"I figure Sam and I will circle around this cabin, hope Donald made himself a couple of windows, and make sure that's where they're at."

"The cars are right in front of you. What more do you need?" Anne Marie insisted, straining again against Jennifer's weight.

She'd like a muzzle about now. And a pair of handcuffs would be useful. Maybe they could lock Anne Marie in the trunk. Just for a little while.

"You all stay put," Sam ordered, reaching up and switching the overhead light so it wouldn't come on. They opened the doors and slipped out into the dark.

Without so much as a goodbye. He could have at least . . . Yeah, well, what did she expect? Sam was scripting his own lines, not Leigh Ann.

It struck Jennifer how sexist the situation seemed, the men going out, armed, to save the day, the women staying behind. She tried to rationalize that there was more to it than gender roles, that she was no good with guns and was the only one available to control Anne Marie, who was now hysterically rabid, and Valerie . . . well, Valerie was seventeen. Somehow none of it washed. The guys were out there, and the women were inside the car. It kind of didn't seem right. Nevertheless, they sat there, in the dark, the blackest kind of country night, following the thin beams of the two flashlights until, a short distance ahead, they separated and then disappeared. That had to be where the cabin was.

If learning to wait graciously was one of life's little lessons, Jennifer had missed it entirely. People she cared about were out there doing who knew what, maybe only seconds from being killed. She wanted to be with them—

even if she got in the way—because somehow it made the whole situation more bearable.

Instead she was stuck in intolerable darkness. She couldn't see the expressions on her companions' faces. Anne Marie, now quiet, seemed to have relaxed some. She no longer strained away from her. Jennifer loosened her grip. Her arms had cramped, more from fear than effort.

Valerie shifted and seemed to lean against her door. She should be all right. It was Anne Marie she was worried about. She'd heard stories about mothers lifting cars to rescue their children. With that kind of adrenaline at her disposal, it was hard to tell what she might do.

Suddenly, a gunshot cracked, and then another, sending a sharp, shooting pain through Jennifer's heart. She could feel the women on either side of her stiffen. And before she realized what was happening, she heard both doors fly open. Suddenly she found herself alone on the backseat, the cool night air blowing past her.

She felt on either side of the seat. Yep. They were both gone. In opposite directions. She should have taken that trunk option while she had it.

At least there'd been no more shots. Not yet. She felt for the small gun Johnny had given her. It was still snug in her pocket.

She scooted across the seat and slipped out onto the grass. The cabin was somewhere ahead, slightly to her left, if she hadn't lost her bearings. That's the direction Sam and Johnny had headed in. If Anne Marie and Valerie went the opposite way, they should be fine. If not . . .

She scurried forward, keeping her hands out in front of her, slipping on the rocks that littered the ground and hugging herself around and past each tree as she came to it. The roots were vicious, her flats catching against them. She didn't know how blind people did it, and she didn't have time to learn.

She heard a loud "Damn it!" a few feet in front of her, and, crouching down, scrambled toward the sound. She stumbled against something soft and fleshy and fell over it. Another oath spewed forth, this one practically in her ear.

Jennifer reached toward the noise, found a mouth, and clamped her hand over it. "You've got to be quiet," she whispered into Anne Marie's ear, then pulled the woman to her feet. Anne Marie shoved her, and she fell back against a tree. Guess Anne Marie wasn't buying into her being in charge.

Jennifer could hear her going forward through the brush. She was right behind Anne Marie and then shifting toward the left. Another step and the world changed. A soft glow radiated from what must have been the front of the cabin because it spilled from one straight, vertical line. Light also poured from a small window, now clearly visible as she came up. Anne Marie, just ahead, crouched on the side of the cabin.

But why light at the front? It was so bright. The question had no more appeared in her head than she could hear someone talking, a deep, throaty, angry voice, a voice she recognized from TV. Paul Collier.

"You did it again, Donald."

Of course. Paul hunted deer. Probably spotlighted deer. He was a man who didn't believe in playing fair.

Jennifer shifted wider to the left, away from the cabin and the small clearing in front of it, well out of range of the light and behind the cover of the trees, so she could get a look at what was going on around front. Her heart caught in her throat. She could see their profiles, Sam standing with his hands clasped behind his head, Johnny with his hands raised as best he could, considering the wound in his shoulder. Their guns lay on the ground in front of them.

The side of Johnny's thigh was seeping blood. Oh, God. And he hadn't even gotten over his last gunshot wound.

Paul, still not visible, continued to talk. "Your daughter," he said sarcastically. "So you had to have your little heart-to-heart. I don't understand it. You had the best possible situation. You didn't bother her; she didn't bother you. Now look at the mess you've made. Again."

"Let them go," another male voice said. Must be Donald. She could see Sam and Johnny, and neither of them were talking. "Let us all go."

She hardly dared to breathe.

"So you can call the police and confess? This isn't just about you anymore, Donald. If that's what you wanted, you should have done it fourteen years ago. Instead you called me. And I helped you. Now you want to repay me by sending me to jail?"

"You shouldn't have had Beverly killed."

"I didn't intend for Beverly to get killed. They were to pick up whatever it was she was going to pass to Zeeman. Guess they got a little overzealous."

"Homicide during the commission of a crime is a felony." Sam.

"Wasn't nothing accidental about Hoffman's death." That one was Johnny.

Jennifer made her way farther out and around, carefully staying far enough away that she was completely out of the light. She could see them all now.

The cabin was a rough shack with only an opening for a door and cinder blocks for steps. Donald stood to the left, Diane half behind him. Paul, on the right, held a mean-looking rifle.

"You can't kill all four of us." Sam's voice. "Surely you don't plan to—"

"I haven't decided. If I were you, I wouldn't push it. No one knows we're out here."

"Actually, that's not true," Sam said.

No, Sam, she thought, hoping he would sense her warning.

"I called the police on the way over."

She allowed herself to breathe. At least he hadn't mentioned that there were three totally unpredictable women lost somewhere in the dark.

"You expect me to believe that?" Paul again.

Sam shrugged as best he could, considering where his hands were. "I don't care what you believe."

"Well, let's say that's true. All the more reason for me to get on with it."

She had to do something fast, but what? She felt for the pistol, and pulled it out of her pocket. Maybe she could shoot out the spotlight. Who was she kidding? She'd fired a gun only once and that was under duress. She'd missed the target entirely and sent everyone around her scrambling for cover. No way she could hit a target like that light from this far away. Besides, she might hit Paul in the process. Or Donald. Or Diane. Or . . . She couldn't chance it, not unless he were actually about to pull the trigger.

Paul raised the rifle.

Jennifer raised the gun.

Abruptly, a barrage of stones poured from the area directly behind Sam and Johnny, pelting Paul's chest just as Jennifer fired the pistol straight into the air, and Anne

Marie emerged from the side of the cabin yelling primitive, warlike whoops at the top of her lungs. As Paul turned in her direction, she caught him in the face with a spray of liquid from what looked like an aerosol can. Then she threw it at his head.

Paul staggered back, dodging stones and clawing at his eyes as the rifle slid to the ground.

They were all over him. Anne Marie, Sam, Donald, Diane—tangled in a mass of arms and legs and bodies. Paul, soundly tackled, lay somewhere beneath.

She could hear his muffled cries. "Get the hell off of me."

No one moved.

By the time Jennifer made it into the circle, Valerie was coming out of the woods, hefting a stone in her right hand.

"Great arm," Jennifer told her.

"All-star pitcher four summers in high school."

"Either one of you got a handkerchief or somethin' I could tie around this leg?" Johnny asked. He sat on the ground seeping blood. Obviously nothing too serious, but enough.

Jennifer pulled off one of her kneesocks and wrapped it around his thigh.

Johnny leaned in and whispered in her ear. "You'll have to come over sometime and let me show you my scars."

She pulled the sock tightly and looped it into a knot. Then she turned and kissed him lightly on the cheek. "You're some partner. You know that?"

He smiled. "Yeah? We're going to have to do something about your shooting skills. I can take you out to the range starting next week. And I think we should enroll you in some kind of martial arts class, maybe karate, or at least get you into some weight training. I know a guy with a gym who—"

She leaned in closer and whispered into his ear. "In case you didn't hear me in the hospital, I quit."

Chapter 39

The solid core door and the dead bolt had been installed in the bedroom of Jennifer's apartment, and the super lock was securely in place on her front door. The hanging ladder had arrived in yesterday's mail. It was time to go home.

"You don't have to leave today," Sam told her as she loaded her cosmetics into a zippered bag, stuffed her toothbrush into its holder, and dumped them all into a box.

"Muffy and I need to get out from under your feet," she said, tossing her toothpaste and floss in with the other things.

"You were never under my feet."

She looked at him. She hated it when he said the right thing. Almost as much as when he didn't. It seemed as if they were breaking up, even though her living there had always been temporary. He hadn't asked her to stay, not permanently, so she had to go. Keeping busy made it easier not to think about it.

She lifted the box and carried it past him, out of the bathroom, dropping it next to the front door. He followed her, as he had all morning while she tried to get her belongings packed up.

Muffy immediately nosed through the box, just in case something edible had fallen in by mistake.

"I'll put some coffee on," Sam offered, heading for the kitchen.

"That would be wonderful." She looked around the room. She must have missed something, but it wasn't as if she were going halfway around the world. She'd only be a few miles away. Sam could bring her whatever she forgot.

"Have you heard from Diane?" he called from behind the partition. She could hear him clinking glassware.

"I spoke with her this morning while you were in the shower. Both she and Anne Marie are hanging in there. She's back at school and plans to stay there. Her teachers have given her plenty of time to make up her work, and the scholarship Donald set up for her is a prepaid, four-year program, so her expenses are all taken care of, regardless of what happens to him."

She squatted down and reached under the chair, searching blindly. She could have sworn Muffy had brought her favorite toy, a green rubber frog. Muffy would be most unhappy if they got home without it.

He poked his head around the divider. "Good thing. I don't think Donald's going to be much help to her for a while. Lots of legal fees. He's got a lot to answer for."

"He told Diane, up at the lake, that when he got to her house in Bethesda, Robert had already shot Colette. He tried to perform CPR, but there was nothing he could do. When Robert realized she was dead, he put the gun to his own head. That's when they struggled, and the gun went off. Donald panicked. He was desperate to get out of the house, but he couldn't very well leave Diane. He found her in an upstairs bedroom, crying, frightened by the noise. The cast on her leg had kept her from getting out of bed by herself. He wrapped her in a blanket and made sure she didn't see anything."

"But why'd he take her to the lake?"

Jennifer sat back on her ankles. That darn frog was definitely lost. "He wanted to explain everything to her before he turned himself in to the police and she read it in the papers. Of course, Paul had other plans."

"Now that she knows who her birth parents are, is that going to make a difference?"

"Myers is arranging a meeting with Mrs. Owens over fall break. She was absolutely ecstatic when she found out we'd located her granddaughter. Anne Marie's being very supportive. Diane even asked her to go with her to Maryland."

She maneuvered forward, on all fours, across to the beanbag. As far as Muffy was concerned, this was a great game, having Jennifer at eye level. She licked her nose. Jennifer pushed her out of the way and lifted up the chair. Nope. Nothing there.

"Diane's eighteen," she said, glancing around the room, "was, as of August fourteenth. She's free to do whatever she wants. Funny how that freedom finally makes you appreciate what your parents do for you." She collapsed with her back against the beanbag and watched as Muffy trotted toward the bedroom.

Sam grinned. "It's tough being a grown-up." He went over to her, offered her his hand, and pulled her up.

"Oh, yeah," she agreed, coming up almost nose-to-nose with him. They broke away: she to the dining table to pack up her computer, he back to the kitchen.

Muffy reappeared, trotting over to her. The frog's head peeked out from the dog's curled lips. "Where in the world did you have that hid? You could have saved me a whole lot of trouble—"

"You talking to me?" Sam called out.

She rubbed Muffy's ears. "You never told me how Paul got the drop on you out at the lake."

Sam returned carrying two cups of coffee. He set one

down for her on the table, and she took a sip. The man did make a decent cup, just the way she liked it, with both cream and sugar.

"Oh, that. Zeeman—"

They heard a knock at the door. Jennifer winced. She'd had enough unexpected company to last her a long time.

Sam opened the door as she unplugged the keyboard and wrapped the cord around it.

"Is Jennifer here?" It was Johnny's voice. What could he possibly want?

Sam, looking somewhat irritated, let him in. He was carrying a large box.

"Marsh," he greeted her, setting the box next to her on the table. "So, looks like you're moving out." He seemed way too pleased, as though somehow he'd won, as if he and Sam were actually in a kind of competition.

The comment irritated her almost enough to make her want to stay. "Johnny. What brings you by?" she asked as nicely as she could, as she coiled the cord from her monitor and secured it with a twist tie.

"You wouldn't let me pay you. . . ." Johnny began.

Sam shot her a look, and she shrugged. It wasn't like she could take money for what she'd done for Diane. It didn't seem right.

"Anyway, I wanted you to have this, a little somethin' to remember me by."

Before she could thank him, he was at the door. Obviously, Johnny was uncomfortable with sentiment. Sam already had his hand on the knob ready to shut it after him, but Johnny stopped, put his palm on the door frame and turned back. "Remember, you need a job, you've got it."

He pulled his hat down and then he was gone. Sam closed the door.

"You shouldn't be accepting gifts from a man like

that," Sam told her. In her mind she could hear Dee Dee and Teri echoing his words.

Well, none of them understood, couldn't understand until they'd stood in an alley with bullets whizzing past. When two people face death together, they develop a certain bond.

She untied the string and lifted the box lid. Inside was a brown felt fedora.

Chapter 40

The zzzzt, zzzzt, zzzzt of the neon light outside the up-stairs window of the Martin & Zimmerman Detective Agency soothed Jimmy with its familiar rhythm. He reached into the bottom drawer of his desk and pulled out another fifth of bourbon, tossing the empty one at the trash can. It hit hard on the floor beside it, but it didn't break.

He unscrewed the top of the new bottle, took a healthy swig, and let out a gasp. It was cheap, but effective. He had all night to nurse that bottle dry, and why not? His partner had left the business, and it was all his fault. He leaned back in the swivel chair, put his feet on his desk, and took another drag on his cigarette. He could feel the smoke reach down into the lowest part of his lungs.

The knock on the door startled him.

"Go away," he called, slurring his words, helping him-self to another gulp of whiskey, and rubbing the thick growth of beard that covered his cheek. He had no use for anybody, hadn't for two days.

Out of the corner of his eye he caught sight of a woman standing in the entrance. He could have sworn he'd locked that door.

He looked her up and down. Tall, thin, lanky, dressed in a form-fitting suit and high heels with legs that went on to meet the sky.

He must be dead because she was an angel.

She flowed over to his desk and tugged the bottle from his grip. "Mr. Zimmerman," she purred, "you've got to help me."

What could an angel want from him?

"I'm out of the business, doll. Go find yourself some other P.I."

"I've got to have the best, Mr. Zimmerman."

He snorted. "The best left out of here two days ago."

"Second best, then," she insisted. A tear ran down her cheek.

Jimmy hated it when women cried. He took his feet down and sat up, as best he could, in his chair. She looked like she needed help, but he was fresh out. "I want you to let yourself out. Then I'm going to drink the rest of that bottle of bourbon you're holding, and hope I'll pass out."

"But—"

"No buts, sweetheart. Now hand it over." He held out his hand.

"But you don't understand . . ."

Jennifer pushed up the brim of the brown fedora and stared at her computer screen. "Okay, Jimmy," she whispered. "If you can solve this one, I'll let you get the girl."

In Conversation...

JUDY FITZWATER AND
JENNIFER MARSH

(Let me preface this interview by saying that I met with a certain amount of hostility when I approached Jennifer about talking with me. As professional as she is about her writing, she harbors some resentment for my playing Watson to her Sherlock. She insists that I'm not always accurate, especially in relating her inner feelings, and complains that I make her seem much more neurotic than she actually is. The fact that I'm published as a result of her adventures and she has yet to see any of her own writing in print remains a sticking point. However, two cappuccinos heavy with whipped cream helped her to warm up to the idea. Plus a promise to ask my editor to review some of her work.)

JUDY: **Jennifer, trouble seems to follow you around. How do the people close to you react to the number of dead bodies that you stumble upon?**

JENNIFER: For heaven's sake, Judy, it's not as if I actually go out looking for corpses. They just sort of find me. Although, I suppose, in the death of literary agent Penney Richmond (which you chronicled in *Dying to Get Published*), I was more of an active participant. Sam was pretty angry about how I got myself mixed up with that one.

JUDY: **Sam's that good-looking investigative newspaper reporter.**

JENNIFER: Right. He works for the *Macon Telegraph*. As I

was saying, he wasn't so understanding, but my coworker Dee Dee (I help her with her catering business) and my whole writers' group—Teri, Leigh Ann, April, and Monique—were behind me all the way. So were Mrs. Walker, an elderly lady I met in Atlanta, and her friends. They knew I couldn't kill that despicable creature Penney, just as I knew Mrs. Walker couldn't have killed her slimy ex-husband Edgar.

JUDY: **I remember. I wrote about Mrs. Walker's troubles in *Dying to Get Even.***

JENNIFER: And then, of course, there's the Diane Robbins case in which I teamed up with private detective Johnny Zeeman, and a woman was shot dead practically in front of us.

JUDY: **Right. That one's *Dying for a Clue*. My third novel.**

JENNIFER: Aren't you the prolific one.

JUDY: **Just answer the questions. Who knows? Some editor might read this and . . .**

JENNIFER: All right. But you make it sound like my involvement with so many murder cases is excessive. Actually, I agree, but I can't seem to do anything about it. You see, in a very real way, murder is my business. I write about it, and, in doing research for my books, I occasionally (Sam would say always) find myself where I shouldn't be.

JUDY: **Selling that first novel is difficult. How do you keep yourself positive, considering the number of rejections you've received?**

JENNIFER: Dwelling on rejections never got anybody anywhere. I've written nine novels, and one of these days I'm actually going to sell one of them. I'm twenty-nine years old, and I've been writing ever since I got out of college. I heard an author speak one time who said, "Persistence is every bit as important as talent." I believe that. Besides, I've got too many years invested to give up now. All I need is that initial break. I figure, after that, I should be able to sell most of what I've written.

So, Judy, who did you say your editor was?

JUDY: **Later.**

JENNIFER: Promise?

JUDY: **It was part of the deal. Your critique group seems to be important to both your personal and professional lives. Do they really help with your writing?**

JENNIFER: Absolutely. I don't know what I'd do without them. They're all very talented, although they do have their problems.

JUDY: **How so?**

JENNIFER: Leigh Ann is a hopeless romantic. She can turn the most innocent encounters into . . . Let's just say she has a vivid imagination. Teri writes romantic suspense. She's a sweetheart, really, but she can seem somewhat brusque to people who don't know her. And those who do. Actually, sometimes she's downright rude. But whenever I've asked her for a favor, she's always come through. Not always the way I might have envisioned it, but she gets the job done. April does children's books. It seems like she's always eating and always pregnant. And one of the gentlest souls I've ever known. And then there's Monique, who keeps a copy of her one published science fiction book on her coffee table. We're not close, but whenever I've really needed her, she's always been there for me. Like family. They're all like family.

JUDY: **Both Leigh Ann and Teri write romance, Monique science fiction, and April children's stories. Can they really help you with your mysteries?**

JENNIFER: They're good writers, all of them, if a little overly dramatic with the prose now and then. We all write popular fiction, which has the same demands regardless of genres: great openings, dynamic characters, and a quick pace. Most important, they're always honest, if not always tactful.

JUDY: **A lot of the people who follow your adventures seem interested in your relationship with Sam. Can you give us an idea what the future may hold for the two of you?**

JENNIFER: I don't like talking about Sam. I care a lot about him, but it's really none of your or anybody else's business.

JUDY: **You haven't figured it out yet, have you?**

JENNIFER: I really haven't. Sometimes we seem so close. But then . . . We just need some time to sort through our feelings and let our relationship develop naturally. Seems like we have more help and advice in that department than we need.

JUDY: **What do you mean?**

JENNIFER: Dee Dee is always trying to get me married off, and Teri and Leigh Ann tell me daily how I shouldn't let a guy like Sam get away. But it seems like every time we try to work out what we are to each other, another crisis comes up.

JUDY: **Or another dead body?**

JENNIFER: Exactly.

JUDY: **Your dog Muffy seems to be a great part of your life. Can you tell us how you came to adopt her?**

JENNIFER: Muffy is a retired racing Greyhound. I got her through one of the Greyhound adoption organizations.

She's terrific. She reminds me there's more to life than writing and work, and she's an absolute sponge for attention. I adore her.

JUDY: **In *Dying to Get Published*, you were arrested. What was it like in jail?**

JENNIFER: I'd prefer not to talk about those few hours I spent incarcerated. Suffice it to say, I never want to go back.

JUDY: **What do you see for yourself in the immediate future?**

JENNIFER: Getting published, of course.

JUDY: **Of course.**

JENNIFER: Now, let's talk about how you made your first sale. And your agent's name. And your editor's.